THE NOW-AND-THEN
DETECTIVE

Other Titles by William Wells

Ride Away Home

Face of the Devil

DETECTIVE JACK STARKEY SERIES

Detective Fiction

The Dollar-A-Year Detective

WILLIAM WELLS

THE NOW-AND-THEN DETECTIVE

A JACK STARKEY MYSTERY

THE PERMANENT PRESS
Sag Harbor, NY 11963

For information, address:
The Permanent Press
4170 Noyac Road
Sag Harbor, NY 11963
www.thepermanentpress.com

Library of Congress Cataloging-in-Publication Data

Wells, William, author.
The now-and-then detective: a Jack Starkey mystery / William Wells.
Sag Harbor, NY: Permanent Press, 2020.
Series: Jack Starkey mysteries; 3
ISBN: 978-1-57962-588-7 (cloth)
    1. Mystery fiction.

PS3623.E4795 N69 2020
813'.6—dc23   2019053162

Printed in the United States of America

"In a real-life whodunit, half the job is figuring out whodunit. The other half is proving it."

—DETECTIVE JACK STARKEY

This book is dedicated to all those detectives who preceded Jack Starkey on the printed page, including, but not limited to, Sherlock Holmes, Sam Spade, Philip Marlowe, Spenser, Travis McGee, Archy McNally, Lucas Davenport, Virgil Flowers, Harry Bosch, Dave Robicheaux, Jack Reacher, Elvis Cole, Hercule Poirot, Columbo, Charlie Chan, and Miss Marple, who have entertained me over the years.

PROLOGUE

Good Old Henry

A May morning, the balmy wind off Lake Michigan bearing the sweet perfume of flowering lilacs, as an old man pushed an empty supermarket cart along a sidewalk on Western Avenue in downtown Lake Forest, Illinois, the cart's wheels bumping and clacking on the cracks and fissures in the concrete.

The man wore a white pin-striped Chicago Cubs home-game jersey with the name "Hartnett" lettered on the back, blue cotton pajama bottoms, brown leather bedroom slippers, and a tweed Sherlock Holmes deerstalker cap, the cap's brim shielding his rheumy brown eyes from the sun. A fringe of white hair was visible beneath the cap; bristles of stubbly hair obtruded from the man's nostrils and ears; his eyebrows grew wild as Scottish gorse. A curious apparition indeed in Lake Forest, one link in the golden chain of commuter towns stretching along Chicago's North Shore, where a vagrant tended to stand out.

Some passing motorists may have wondered about this man with momentary curiosity: Did grandpa wander away from a nursing home between head counts? But to the town folk who knew him, he was just good old Henry Wilberforce, recently eccentric in this manner, out and about on one of his quixotic errands.

A black-and-white-striped railroad crossing gate descended across Western Avenue, red lights flashing, bell clanging, announcing the arrival of the southbound 8:07 Metra commuter train at Lake Forest Station. Henry stopped to watch.

"You know, Buddy," Henry said, "when I was a young man, I rode the 7:10 every weekday morning into the city. Father believed public transportation, and not limousines or fancy cars, was more appropriate for someone my age on his way to work. He was driven to the office in his limo."

Although no Buddy, or anyone else, could be seen with Henry, Buddy answered, "Yes, I know."

The train creaked and groaned to a stop, its air brakes whooshing, and its doors slid open for the men and women in business attire waiting on the platform. They stepped up into the line of silver-sided, double-deck Metra cars.

"Look at them, Buddy," Henry said. "Foot soldiers in Chicago's vast army of commerce! Ha! Got my honorable discharge from that outfit many years ago." He smiled. "Used to be hog butchering, tool making, wheat stacking in my day. City of Big Shoulders. I could recite that Carl Sandburg poem as a boy, all of it; Father had me do it at dinner parties to amuse the guests. What they do in the city now is shout at one another in the commodity pits, and move money around with computers while sitting in their high-rise offices. Nobody actually makes anything anymore."

Buddy answered, "Yes, I know."

As the train lumbered out of the station, a Lake Forest police cruiser pulled up to the curb and parked. The driver, Sgt. Stan Kowalski, powered down the window and greeted Henry with a smile: "Morning there, Mr. Wilberforce." Taking note of the shopping cart, he asked, "On your way to the grocery store?"

Henry nodded and said, "Yes, Sergeant Stan. I need a few items."

He stood erect, put his hands on his hips, tilted back his head, filled his lungs, and said, "It's a fine day to be alive, that's for sure."

"Considering the alternative," Sgt. Stan responded. Their usual repartee.

"Say hi to Sergeant Stan, Buddy," Henry said.

Sgt. Stan knew the drill; he looked down at the sidewalk beside Henry, nothing there, and said, "Hi there, Buddy. Nice day for a walk." He knew that Buddy was the name of Henry's golden retriever who'd died at a ripe old age many years ago. Whatever gets you through the day, the sergeant reflected.

"I heard about all that money you gave the city to fix up the town beach," he said. "That was real nice of you."

"It was?" Henry responded. "Well, I don't seem to remember that."

Driving up, Sgt. Stan had noticed the name on the back of Henry's Cubs jersey. "Who's Hartnett?" he asked.

"Oh, that's Gabby Hartnett, the starting catcher. Looks to me like a future Hall of Famer."

"Huh. What happened to Contreras?"

"Now there's the mystery," Henry said. "In the game yesterday, this Hartnett fellow was behind the plate without any explanation."

Sgt. Stan, who worshiped at Saint Leo's and Wrigley Field, knew for certain that Willson Contreras was the team's starting catcher. He also knew that the team's schedule showed an off day yesterday, with no game that Henry could have seen. He eased the cruiser away from the curb, saluted, and called out, "Take 'er easy, Mr. W!"

"Only way to take 'er, Sergeant Stan," Henry replied, clicking his slippered heels together as he returned the sergeant's salute in the British army manner, palm out and vibrating. Then he said, "Let's move along, Buddy, we need the exercise."

Henry arrived at the Jewel Supermarket, a single-story red-brick building three blocks north of the train station on Western. He guided his cart through the automatic entrance doors, one of which had a sign on it reading "Service Dogs Only" and exchanged greetings with the checkout ladies, baggers, and shelf stockers as he headed to aisle three, canned fruits and vegetables. Buddy was not a service dog, but he could go anywhere he pleased, being invisible to everyone but his master, including into this supermarket.

Henry moved along the aisle, Buddy at his side, selecting only certain brands of green beans (whole, sliced, dilled, French and Italian cuts), garbanzo beans, wax beans, lima beans, kidney beans, baked beans, peas of regular and baby diameter, beets (plain, pickled, and Harvard), mushrooms (whole, and pieces and stems), corn (regular and creamed), spinach, artichokes, mixed vegetables, asparagus, sauerkraut, carrots, okra, pearl onions, white potatoes, squash, tomatoes, peaches, pears, mandarin oranges, pineapple, cranberry sauce (jellied and whole berry), applesauce (regular, chunky, and chunky with cinnamon), apricots, blueberries, cherries, grapefruit sections, and fruit cocktail, all delivered from field to truck to canning factory to truck again to grocery shelf to the dining tables of the nation and the world, a cornucopian production line that Henry knew as well as anything in his life.

From one pass down the aisle, the cart was packed to overflowing and now too heavy for Henry to push. That was the signal for Bob Buehler, the store manager, his starched tan jacket bearing the Jewel logo, reading glasses hanging from a cord around his neck, who had been watching, to round up four of his employees. One took over Henry's cart and headed it toward the checkout lanes while the others lined up behind Henry with empty carts. Bob watched this parade, calling in reinforcements as needed. In this fashion, Henry led them throughout the store, pointing out items, again always specific brands, with which his Jewel squad filled their carts.

It turned out to be a seven-cart day. As Henry stood chatting with Bob about sports—Bob not asking about Hartnett because Bob was a White Sox man and didn't know from Cubs—and weather and politics, the groceries moved along the conveyor belts of three checkout stations that had been closed to other shoppers, some of whom, not having witnessed this scene before, glared and huffed with annoyance until Bob handed them coupons applicable to various products. There was some swapping of coupons as the shoppers attempted to match the discounts with items actually in their baskets.

The checkout nearly complete, Henry found his Bank of Lake Forest debit card in the rear pocket of his pajama bottoms and handed it to Bob, who swiped it through the three card machines.

Then he presented Henry with three receipts to sign totaling $880.42. The baggers did not ask, "Paper or plastic?" Instead, they loaded Henry's groceries back into the carts.

Leaving the groceries behind, Henry pulled an empty cart from the lineup, and headed for the door.

"Always a pleasure, Mr. Wilberforce!" Bob called out to his best customer. "See you next time!"

Henry acknowledged with a nod and a wave as he pushed the cart outside. He looked over at the base of an elm tree growing in the strip of grass between the sidewalk and the street.

"There's a good spot to relieve yourself, Buddy boy," Henry said, and Buddy did.

Inside, Bob Buehler ordered Henry's groceries to be restocked. He would mail a store check in the amount of $880.42, as Henry had instructed him to do when he began these shopping trips three months ago, to the Our Lady of Grace Food Bank in Waukegan, a blue-collar city nine miles and a world away to the north, their being, so far as anyone knew, no hungry people in Lake Forest.

Back at police headquarters, Sgt. Stan was curious about whether Gabby Hartnett existed only in Henry's mind, like Buddy, his dog. A computer search led him to the information that Hartnett was behind the plate for the Chicago Cubs from 1922 to 1941, when Henry was a boy. Hartnett was enshrined in the Baseball Hall of Fame at Cooperstown in 1955.

The sergeant shook his head and thought: *Good old Henry sure is one unique piece of work these days.*

1.

The Corpse in Question

It was the third week of October and I was feeling lucky because I'd just dodged another bullet. This time, it was not the hot-lead kind, it was a Category 3 hurricane named Irena. Twelve days earlier, Irena, who was definitely not a lady, delivered only a glancing blow to Fort Myers Beach, the small town on Florida's Southwest Gulf Coast where I lived, and then spun northward up the Gulf of Mexico toward the Florida Panhandle.

We lost a lot of trees, power was out for a few days, there was some flooding, and damage to roofs, mobile homes, and structures not built to modern building codes, and tiki huts on the beach blew to Iowa, but no one was reported killed or injured and everyone felt very lucky that we'd been spared the devastation that people living in Panhandle towns like Apalachicola, Fort Walton Beach, and Pensacola had suffered.

Winston Churchill said, "Nothing in life is so exhilarating as to be shot at without result." Got that right.

I was sitting in a folding aluminum lawn chair on the rear deck of *Phoenix*, my houseboat, moored at Salty Sam's Marina on Estero Bay, which had provided safe harbor from the storm, having a morning cup of coffee and reading the sports pages of the *Fort Myers News-Press*, when my pal Cubby Cullen, the Fort Myers Beach police chief, called me on my cell phone and offered to buy me lunch. Cubby was, shall we say, penurious, so whenever he offered to pick up a check it meant he wanted something in return.

I met Cubby at Captain Mack's Seafood Shack on the Caloosahatchee River, one of my favorite restaurants, where I always got the fried shrimp roll with onion rings. Everything tasted better when battered and deep fried. Cubby was of the same epicurean opinion.

Clarence "Cubby" Cullen was a short, portly man with a round face, in his mid-fifties, who resembled a teddy bear. Apparently he always had, because he picked up that nickname as a boy. But his appearance was deceptive. Cubby had been an army ranger, and the deputy chief of the Toledo, Ohio, police department before he retired to Florida with his wife, Mable, got bored playing golf and fishing, and applied for the Fort Myers Beach chief's job when the former chief drowned in a boating accident. I met him when he became a regular at The Drunken Parrot, the bar I own, and we sometimes fished and went to the police shooting range together.

As we waited for our food, Cubby and I chatted about the hurricane damage, sports, and politics, and then, knowing that he had something else on his mind, I finally asked, "So, Cubby, what's up?"

"Ten days ago, a man from Lake Forest, Illinois, near Chicago, was murdered in his winter home in Naples," Cubby told me. "The police chief, a man named Tom Sullivan, called me yesterday. He knows that you worked with the Naples Police Department, before he started there, on another homicide case."

I knew what was coming.

"Tom asked if you would talk to him about this murder," Cubby said.

To which I replied, "That last case involved a serial killer, Cubby. But one murder? . . . They've got detectives. Why do they need me?"

Cubby took a bite of his fried shrimp roll, cocktail sauce dripping onto his white uniform shirt, and said, "This one's got some very sensitive aspects, Jack. The corpse in question is a guy named

Henry Wilberforce. Murdered in his sleep. Naples PD has positioned the killing publicly as a burglary gone bad, and maybe it was, but Sullivan thinks that Henry might have been targeted. And Tom Sullivan knows his stuff."

"And who was this Henry . . . ?"

"Wilberforce. He was a billionaire known for his generous philanthropy," Cubby explained. "The newspaper stories about his death didn't appear on the sports pages, and you don't watch TV news, so I'm not surprised you haven't heard about it."

"I've never gotten into trouble reading the sports pages," I said.

"Granted, but sometimes trouble just comes a-knockin' on Jack Starkey's door," Cubby said, speaking the God's honest truth.

"I don't know if I want to take on another case," I said. "I'll have to think about that."

I noticed that Cubby was looking at my plate.

"Are you going to finish your onion rings?" he asked.

I was going to, but I pushed my plate toward him and said, "Feel free, Cubby my man. You're paying for 'em."

I retired from the Chicago Police Department's Homicide Division after being shot three times, once while a United States Marine and twice while on the City of Chicago's payroll. It took me a while, but eventually I got the point: Detective Jack Starkey had enough holes in his hide and would do well to become Private Citizen Jack Starkey while he was still ambulatory and reasonably lucid.

I noticed that Cubby was smiling, as if enjoying some private joke. And he was, because, by the time Captain Mack's world-class key lime pie arrived, I had pretty much decided it was time for another jolt of the excitement that came from the hunt for a killer.

Cubby just kept on smiling that enigmatic Mona Lisa smile, because he knew I'd agree to talk to Sullivan, and where that talk would lead. So did I. Have you read Joseph Conrad's *Heart of Darkness*?

"Okay, Cubby, I'll at least talk to Tom Sullivan about his case," I said. "As a favor to you."

Cubby was looking at my pie plate. A few bites left. I slid the plate over to him and said, "Next time we go dutch."

So that's how my next adventure in the world of murder and mayhem began. If a detective agrees to just look at a case, he's hooked. It's like going to an animal shelter, just to look at the inmates. You don't go home alone.

The waitress came over and put the check onto the table between us. Cubby picked it up, winked at me, and said, "Tell Tom Sullivan he owes me lunch."

Naples was one of those sparkling, twenty-carat enclaves of wealth and privilege, like Palm Beach, but lower key, where 1-per-centers bought multimillion-dollar estates to shelter them from the winter storms of the north. See something you like? If you have to ask the price, you can't afford it. You could fire a cannon down Fifth Avenue South, the main drag, and not hit a Democrat. *We're not in Wrigleyville anymore, Toto*, is a thought I had during my first visit. So the fact that the late Henry Wilberforce was a billionaire who was generous with his money didn't, on its face, make him much different from a great many of the city's other inhabitants.

The best definition of wealth I'd ever heard was that, if you had enough money to support the lifestyle you chose, you had it made in the shade. You were a resident of Fat City. Rolling in clover. A winner in the game of life. The trick was to choose a lifestyle your skill set could support. For example, a retired Chicago homicide detective like myself should not try to live like Johnny Depp. Nor, as it turned out, should Johnny Depp.

As a full-time detective, my skill set involved solving murders, so I didn't expect to live in a mansion with a water view, or drive a Bentley, or fly private. Overreaching bred unhappiness. While on the job in ChiTown, I found contentment by carrying a badge and a gun. I played the hand I was dealt, day to day, as well as I could, and, for me, that was enough. Win some, lose some, suck it up and soldier on, and, as the great philosopher Satchel Paige said, "Don't look back. Something might be gaining on you."

Most male cops I knew had a retirement dream of one kind or another. Golf, fishing, hunting, world travel, season tickets to the home team, and beer in the cooler were common elements. Sitting in a rocking chair on a porch, flipping playing cards into a hat, with the bass jumping on the lake, would not be out of the question. Nor would a good cigar. I imagine that female cops had their own version of the dream, but I never asked—maybe because one of them might say, "I want to spend my golden years with a man the exact opposite of you, Jack." Which, sad to say, wouldn't have surprised me one iota.

My retirement dream, concocted during endless stakeouts, involved living in a warm climate, and maybe, if lucky, owning a bar and residing on a boat. Which, as it turned out, was exactly what I did. I found the warm climate in Florida. My bar was The Drunken Parrot. Some might think it odd for a recovering alcoholic to own a bar. I justified it by telling myself that I could still enjoy the conviviality without the liquor, plus, it was a good business in a spring-break town.

Sometimes I'd walk into a bar, never the one I owned, slide up onto a stool, and tell the barkeep to give me a double shot of Black Jack and a mug of beer, Goose Island if they had it, brewed in my hometown Chicago, and if not, then whichever. I'd drop the shot glass into the beer mug and watch it descend to the bottom, the two liquids of different viscosity not blending. Back in the day, my next move would be to down the drink in one swallow, feeling the anesthetic warmth which, I erroneously believed, was an antidote for the PTSD effect of murder investigations. But that was then and this was now, so I'd signal the barkeep and also order a diet root beer, my current drink of choice. When I was done, I'd slap a twenty onto the bar and leave, still sober after nine years.

My home was named *Phoenix*, a houseboat that was more house than boat. It was seaworthy at one time, but that time was in the rearview mirror. So was a certain amount of my own seaworthiness. I named my boat after the bird of Greek mythology which rose from its own ashes. When I moved to Florida, I had the same thing in mind.

My Chicago PD disability checks were supplemented by my bar's profits, and by income I got from my friend Bill Stevens, a *Chicago Tribune* police reporter who wrote a series of best-selling novels based upon my detective career. His fictional detective was named Jack Stoney. Bill gave me a generous percentage of his book royalties, and he paid me to edit his manuscripts to make certain he got the cop stuff right.

For example, in an early draft of one of his books, Bill wrote that Beretta had the US Army's contract to provide its M9 9mm service pistol as the sidearm for the troops. In fact, by then, Beretta had lost that contract, which it had had since 1985, to the Sig Sauer M17, a variant of its Model P320. I made the correction. Gun people were very precise in their firearms knowledge. For obvious reasons, you didn't want to get on their bad side.

Bill was also my silent partner in The Drunken Parrot. He could easily have retired on the book royalties, but he said that being a police reporter kept his head in the crime game, which informed his writing.

As icing on my retirement cake, I was in a long-term relationship with a lovely and intelligent Cuban-American woman named Marisa Fernandez de Lopez. My wife, Claire, divorced me when I was a detective with a drinking problem. Or maybe a drinker with a detective problem. In those days, I would have divorced me too. Marisa was my second chance at having a significant romantic relationship. According to Sammy Cahn and Jimmy Van Heusen, as interpreted by the late, great Francis Albert Sinatra, "Love is lovelier the second time around." I didn't know about that, but I could say with certainty that it was better than dining alone.

In summary: Retired in a warm climate, owned a bar, lived on a boat, had an amazing lady friend, was immortalized in crime fiction, and, despite being shot at more than once, still on the right side of the grass. Every morning, I looked at a rich man in my shaving mirror.

However, there was one caveat. My previous life as a homicide detective had a certain edginess to it. I'd felt a rush of adrenaline in my bloodstream when I found myself in a situation where a positive outcome was not assured. To my surprise, I discovered that life in paradise could sometimes become a bit . . . boring. Which was why, now and then, I missed my old life, had twice agreed to consult with local police departments on homicide investigations, and why I decided to do it again.

Now and then.

That was the key.

More often would have felt like work.

2.

God Has Left the Building

I was scheduled to meet with Naples Police Chief Tom Sullivan in his office at eleven A.M. I had enough of getting up at zero-dark-thirty in the marines, and as a detective, so I always tried to not commit to anything more complicated than coffee and a shower before ten. The memory of my Parris Island drill instructor running into the squad bay at five A.M., banging two garbage can lids together, and shouting, "Okay scumbags, drop your cocks and grab your socks, the work day has begun!" was as fresh as a spring bouquet.

I was awakened at seven thirty by the drumming of a hard rain on *Phoenix*'s metal roof. Soon, the rainy season would end, replaced by winter drought and brushfires. It's always something. I noticed that my roommate, Joe, was also awake. He was a stray cat named after my brother, a Chicago fireman who'd been killed trying to save a little boy's dog from a burning tenement. The dog survived.

Joe the cat hopped aboard *Phoenix* one day four years ago while I was sitting on the deck, drinking a diet root beer and listening to a Tampa Bay Rays baseball game on the radio. He had the chewed ears and other battle scars of a street fighter. He stared at me, meowed, found a bit of shade, curled up, just like he owned the place, and went to sleep. We've been together ever since.

I got out of bed, padded barefoot into the galley, followed by Joe, started the Mr. Coffee machine, put a strawberry Pop-Tart into the toaster, and opened a can of tuna for Joe. Then I picked up a FedEx box lying on the counter, found a red pen in a drawer, took out the manuscript of Bill Stevens's new novel, *Stoney's Downfall*, sat at the galley table, and began to read.

I was confident that Jack Stoney would, in the end, avoid said downfall, because he needed to be around for Bill's next book. Bill made his fictional detective taller, tougher, and a better marksman than I am. But I didn't mind. The vagaries and doldrums of real life don't sell books.

Chapter One of *Stoney's Downfall* began this way:

Det. Lt. Jack Stoney sat with his feet up on his battered metal desk in the homicide squad room on a Monday morning, reading the Chicago Tribune, *sipping coffee from a Styrofoam cup, and nibbling a powdered-sugar doughnut, the white residue snowing down onto his black shirt front.*

Sweet Jumpin' Jesus, Stoney said to himself as he read a page-one story bylined Bill Stevens. More people were shot and wounded or killed in the city over the hot summer weekend than all last month in Afghanistan and Iraq combined. We should get combat pay on top of the chump-change salary the city gives us to risk our lives every friggin' day, he reflected.

It was common knowledge that a growing number of patrol officers wouldn't even venture into certain neighborhoods on the South or West Sides of the city after dark, even in cruisers and wearing Kevlar vests, with shotguns and automatic rifles at the ready. Up-armored Humvees were what was needed, but there was no budget for that, Stoney knew, because the pols stole so much moola from the city coffers.

He noticed the captain in charge of the Detective Division's Homicide Section, a guy named Tony Bryce, come out of his office holding a black loose-leaf notebook and head toward his desk. It was never good news when the captain came toward you holding a murder book. Bryce wasn't that bad of a guy, truth be told, but if he was going to give you a murder book to work it meant someone else had already fucked it up. A new assignment came verbally, with no paperwork started yet.

"Sorry to interrupt you reading the comics pages, Jack, but I've got a matter needs your attention," Bryce said.

He dropped the loose-leaf notebook onto Stoney's desk with a plop.

"Haven't gotten to the comics yet," Stoney said. "Main news is funny enough, if you have a perverted sense of humor."

"Got that right," Bryce said. "Anyhow, you've heard about that priest from Holy Innocents Parish who was killed last month."

"Yeah," Stoney said. "He was an accused pedophile, found in the church rectory, cock cut off and stuffed into his mouth, premortem, they said, and shot in the heart."

"The irony that a pedophile priest headed up a parish named Holy Innocents not being lost on us," Bryce commented.

"I thought Kozlowski caught that case," Stoney said, putting his feet down onto the floor.

He looked around the squad room. Koz wasn't there or Bryce would have called Stoney into his office and closed the door.

"Stan was assigned to the case," Bryce said. "Word just came down from on high that certain people have a problem with his investigation. Certain people including the mayor and the archbishop and, for all I know, the friggin' Pope in Rome."

Stoney knew that Bryce hated face-to-face confrontations. He probably called Koz at home that morning and gave him the news that he was off the case. Maybe Koz was having breakfast at The Baby Doll Polka Lounge, a favorite cop hangout, his usual breakfast being Black Jack neat with a beer back.

"Any suspects?" Stoney asked.

Bruce tapped the murder book. "It's all in here."

"Give me the executive summary."

"The leading suspect is a guy whose son was allegedly abused by Father Sean Ferguson."

"And the problem with that is?" Stoney asked.

"Is that the suspect is a prominent businessman and major donor to the Democratic party. So the brass wants someone else to have done it, if at all possible."

I wasn't surprised that Bill's new story involved the sexual abuse scandal rocking the Catholic Church worldwide. His sister's son in Pittsburgh was one of the abuse victims. Bill told me about that during his last visit to Fort Myers Beach for some tarpon fishing. He said that, once the Pittsburgh priest was publicly identified, he would go there and kill him. Apparently by slicing off his dork, stuffing it into his pie hole, then shooting him in the ticker.

But, of course, Bill would never actually do that. Instead, he got his revenge by writing a book about it. I didn't know for certain if the pen was mightier than the pruning shears the killer used on Father Sean Ferguson's ding-dong, but I hoped the book would help shine the purifying rays of sunlight onto a church that had lost its moral authority by betraying its flock over so many past decades.

My family had always been steadfast Catholics, but I decided, after the first abuse scandal was uncovered by the *Boston Globe*, and more and more cases came to light, to never set foot in a church again, and I had not. You didn't need to enter a building with an altar, rows of wooden pews, stained glass windows, and the aroma of burning incense wafting in the air to find God.

Maybe, in at least some churches around the world, God, like Elvis, had left the building.

Marisa attended Saint Leo's every Sunday. "It's my church too," she once told me. "They can't take it away from me."

Without her knowing, I checked out the parish priest, Father Rafael Sandoval. I found out that he was a retired Marine Corps chaplain. I went to the church and introduced myself.

"Marisa has talked about you," he said. "I completely understand why you don't come here with her."

"I appreciate that, Father," I said. "I own a bar called The Drunken Parrot. I invite you to worship there whenever the Spirit moves you."

After that conversation, the Spirit moved Father Sandoval every Sunday after his church services and whenever he wanted to watch a soccer game on our big-screen TVs. And sometimes when no game was on. On his first Sunday at the bar, I introduced him all around and Sam poured him a double shot of Jose Cuervo. He raised his glass in a toast: "May you be in Heaven half an hour before the Devil knows you're dead."

A good sentiment indeed.

3.

The Case of the Dead Philanthropist

The rain had stopped, replaced by bright sunlight in an azure sky. You don't like the weather in the subtropics, just wait a moment. I drove from Fort Myers Beach to Naples. Police headquarters were located in a one-story stone building at 355 Riverside Circle. I'd been there many times during my earlier work with the Naples Police Department, under a previous chief, Wade Hansen, who was now the mayor.

The grounds were nicely landscaped with trees, bushes, and flowers whose names Marisa knew. I'm not suggesting that real men didn't know botany, I'm just saying that I did not. But ask me anything about firearms, classic cars, major league baseball, or the precise ingredients of a Chicago-style hot dog, and I'm your guy.

I pulled into the parking lot and waited for the song playing on my car sound system to end. The song was Nelson Riddle's "Theme from Route 66," *Route 66* being a classic TV series of the early 1960s, which I watched on a cable channel featuring old programs. For me, the star of the show was not Martin Milner as Tod Stiles or George Maharis as Buz Murdock—why no second "d" on Tod and second "z "on Buz I never knew—it was the car they drove along the fabled highway, a sweet Corvette like mine.

When the song ended, I killed the engine, got out, walked through the front entrance doors of the HQ building, and into a large, circular lobby. I approached a female civilian receptionist seated behind a glass partition. She said, through an amplified round metal porthole, "Good morning, sir, how may I help you?"

At my old precinct house in Chicago, you were greeted by a grizzled, cigar-chomping desk sergeant named Howard Steinhouse who was protected, not by bulletproof glass, but by the .45-caliber Smith & Wesson on his hip, and who would just as soon shoot you as help you if he didn't like your looks. I'm certain he kept our caseload down.

"I'm Jack Starkey," I told the young woman, who looked to be not long out of high school. "I have an appointment with Chief Sullivan."

She said, "His office is through those doors. You'll see a sign. And you have a nice day, sir."

I smiled and said, "You have a nice day too." I didn't tell her that I was there to help solve a murder because I didn't want to rain upon her nice day. In my experience, civilians don't think that a murder investigation is as exciting as I do.

I went through the doors as instructed and followed the sign down the hallway to the left, and came to a door labeled "Office of Police Chief Thomas Sullivan." I walked into the reception area where another young woman, this one wearing a police uniform, was seated behind a desk. There was a red leather sofa, matching side chairs, a glass coffee table, and oil paintings of tropical scenes on the walls. The coffee table held copies of old magazines like *Sports Illustrated*, *Field & Stream*, and *Guns & Ammo*. That reminded me of the old-time barbershop I went to in Fort Myers Beach where haircuts were fifteen bucks and you could smoke a cigar if you had a mind to.

I'd dressed for the occasion in a blue blazer over a white oxford-cloth shirt with a button-down collar, open at the neck, khaki slacks, and black loafers. My usual workday attire being a tee shirt, jeans, and running shoes. Someone's going to cut you a paycheck, you dress up.

During my first visit to Naples, to dine at one of the city's fancy-schmantzy restaurants with Marisa, I felt a bit self-conscious, a fish out of water, a kid from Wrigleyville among the swells. Maybe the maître d' would look me over and say, with a sneer, "Deliveries to the rear." But he didn't. Maybe he thought I was the lovely and elegant Marisa's bodyguard. She certainly had a body worth guarding.

"Chief Sullivan is expecting you, Mr. Starkey," the receptionist said, before I could tell her my name. Either she was a psychic, or the woman downstairs had alerted her. I hoped it was the latter, because, if she could read my thoughts, she would know I was thinking that no other cop I'd come across filled out a uniform like she did. Inappropriate, perhaps, but, as Brother Timothy, one of my Loyola University professors, used to tell us, a man can't control his thoughts, only his deeds. Marisa and I had an exclusive relationship, but that didn't mean she couldn't cast an appreciative eye upon those shirtless spring break college boys with six-pack abs frolicking on the sand. Or that I didn't notice the girls in string bikinis playing beach volleyball. No harm, no foul.

"I'll show you to Chief Sullivan's office," Officer Knockout told me, and I followed her down a hallway and into a large corner office with an open door.

"Chief, this is Mr. Starkey," she said to a man seated behind a desk.

"Thank you, Cathy," Tom Sullivan said as he stood and walked around the desk toward me.

He was about forty-five, tall, with short brown hair, a neatly trimmed mustache, and the lean build of an athlete who'd stayed in shape. He was wearing a uniform consisting of a crisp white shirt with a gold badge, dark blue pants, and black shoes polished to a high shine. I knew from Googling him that he'd graduated from West Point, served as an army infantry officer, and then did twenty years with the Philadelphia Police Department before taking the Naples job. A man, clearly, of discipline and competence. I assumed that he'd Googled me, too, and knew that I'd played baseball at Loyola, served six years as a Marine Corps officer, and then fourteen years with the Chicago PD.

Two old soldiers with a murder to solve. As one of my Chicago colleagues used to say, "That's about as much fun as you can have with your clothes on."

He offered a firm handshake and said, "Jack, I'm Tom Sullivan. I appreciate you agreeing to meet with me about our murder case."

He gestured toward a grouping of furniture near the windows and said, "Please, have a seat and I'll tell you what I know. Were you offered coffee, or something else to drink, or a doughnut?"

I hadn't been, but told him I had, and declined. I didn't want to get the young officer in the reception area charged with dereliction of duty. Maybe I'd ask her for a doughnut on the way out.

"I'm told by Mayor Hansen that you helped us with a case a few years ago and did excellent work," Sullivan said. "If you choose to help us again, the same fee will apply."

That fee had been generous, a lot more than the dollar Cubby Cullen paid me for helping him on my last homicide case.

In that case, an assassin had skillfully made all six deaths appear to be from natural causes, and the fact that they were not was never made public. It was a truly bizarre investigation. Three old men, bored in retirement from high-paying careers, decided to even scores around town by hiring a Miami hit man who'd almost succeeded in adding me to his murderous roster.

Sullivan said, "The murder of Henry Wilberforce has already been in the news. He was a prominent person, being a billionaire and a generous charitable donor, very well-known here."

"Cubby Cullen said you've told the public that the murder happened during a random burglary, but you really believe that the victim was targeted," I said. "And you don't want the real killer to know you're after him."

"Right. Mr. Wilberforce, who was eighty-two, was the heir to a big Chicago company called Wilberforce Foods. He was found shot once in the forehead with a .22-caliber bullet while asleep in bed in his canal-front mansion in the Port Royal neighborhood."

I'd heard of Wilberforce Foods, one of Chicago's biggest companies. Its name was on food products in grocery stores. I should check to see if they made Pop-Tarts. Maybe I'd be granted a lifetime supply if I solved the case.

"What about Henry's wife?" I asked Sullivan.

"Miriam Wilberforce died about ten years ago from a fall down a stairway in their Lake Forest, Illinois, house. Their son, Peter, was a marine officer killed in a helicopter crash. Henry and Miriam had been winter residents of Naples for more than thirty years. The Lake Forest police chief told my detective via a phone call that, for the past several years, Mr. Wilberforce has been behaving strangely."

"What do you mean by behaving strangely?" I asked.

"He was said to walk around town wearing costumes, mixing up the past with the present, and talking to an imaginary dog named Buddy."

"Sounds like a rather common case of dementia," I said. "Not unusual for an older person, much less someone who was eighty-two."

"Yes, but here's the unusual part. Henry and Miriam's charitable foundation made generous gifts for many years. But recently, my detective was told, Henry had also been giving major gifts to people and institutions, apparently randomly. You might have heard about his gift of three million dollars to build housing for migrant workers in Immokalee, and for a Naples day care center for their children. It made national news. And a lot more such gifts up in Lake Forest."

I had not heard about that. If he'd have paid for a major refurbishing of Wrigley Field, I would have taken note.

"How did people react to gifts like that?" I asked Sullivan.

"It was known that Mr. Wilberforce suffered a mild stroke, in Lake Forest, just before his odd behavior began, and that he had good days and bad days. His butler and cook, Franz and Anna Mueller, took care of him, and neighbors and the local police kept an eye out, so no one worried about his well-being."

"Tell me about the gift giving here," I said.

"For years, the Wilberforce Foundation was a major supporter of Naples cultural institutions," Sullivan said. "But, beginning a year or so ago, there were reports about him doing things like finding a stray dog and giving a million dollars to the Collier County Humane Society. Setting up a college fund for the son of his lawn man. Buying a Range Rover for a guy who delivered pizzas to his house while driving some sort of old car. Things like that. Mayor Hansen considered Henry to be a very special person. A pillar of the community. A pillar who also gave money to the mayor's campaigns. He wants the killer apprehended, and soon."

I felt confident about apprehending the killer, but not so much about the soon part.

"You can take the murder book with you," Sullivan told me. "Look it over and let me know what you think."

"I assume one of your detectives started the book," I said.

"Right. A young woman named Allie Duncan."

"Won't Detective Duncan resent me taking over her case?" I asked.

"Allie got her gold shield only five months ago," Sullivan said. "She doesn't mind that we're taking advantage of your experience. She thinks she can learn from you."

Reality check: In the real world, one-third of all murder cases were not solved. My close rate was better than that, but no one bats a thousand. Ted Williams, the greatest hitter in the history of baseball, with a lifetime average of .344, failed at the plate 65.6 percent of the time.

Just as Sullivan and I were finishing, Wade Hansen, the mayor, who was police chief when I first worked with the Naples department, appeared in the doorway, came in, and shook my hand.

"Good to have you with us again, Jack," he said.

"Happy to help out."

"Can you believe a hit man in our town again?" he asked. "This isn't friggin' Miami."

"I'll do my best, but no guarantees," I told him.

"No guarantees needed. Your best is enough."

Hansen left and as I stood to depart, Sullivan said, "One more thing, Jack."

He opened a desk drawer, took out a black leather case, and handed it to me. I flipped it open and saw it held a Naples Police Department gold detective's shield. I put the case into the inside pocket of my sport coat. Truth be told, I never felt fully dressed without a badge and a gun.

"We can issue you one of our 9mm Berettas, but maybe you'd rather use your own handgun," Sullivan said.

I nodded, shook his hand, and said, "My Glock and I have been through a lot, so I'll stick with it."

And just like that, I was off and running with The Case of the Dead Philanthropist. It would prove to be as complex and challenging as any I'd ever had.

4.

Professor Jack Starkey

"Say more about how you're partnering with a young female detective," Marisa commented while we were having dinner that night at the Tarpon Lodge on Pine Island in the Gulf of Mexico. "You like women and you like guns. A woman with a gun seems an irresistible combo. Do you have a photo of her I can see?"

Ten years younger than I am, Marisa had lustrous, shoulder-length black hair, sparkling dark eyes, and a body that turned heads, which she kept fit by running marathons and practicing power yoga. She owned a real estate agency in Fort Myers Beach that did well enough for her to live in one of the waterfront estates she bought and sold for her clients, but she preferred her cozy Key West style pink stucco cottage on Mango Street in Fort Myers Beach. Sometimes, after a nice dinner she cooked, I spent the night at her house. She rarely spent the night aboard *Phoenix*, saying it was "unsuitable for civilized habitation." "But you found it," I said. "For you, not me," she said.

"I haven't met her yet," I told Marisa. "And she's not my partner. She's more of an assistant on the case."

"Ready to cater to your every need?" she asked with a raised eyebrow and impish grin.

"I wouldn't characterize her help as catering," I said. "She's new to the job, and the Naples police chief said she wants to learn from me."

"Professor Jack Starkey," Marisa said. "How very nice. You'll need a tweed sport coat and bow tie."

It was a warm evening, the stars shining in a clear sky, the moon full, as we sat at a table on the lodge's front porch. It was one of our favorite restaurants.

"So where are you with your investigation?" Marisa asked as our food arrived.

After meeting with Sullivan, I had driven back to Fort Myers Beach, stopped at my houseboat to change out of my dress-up clothes, and fed Joe a can of salmon for lunch. Then I took the Naples murder book to The Drunken Parrot. I'd checked in with Sam Longtree, a Seminole Indian who was my bartender, sat in a booth with a burger and a diet root beer, and read the murder book before attending to some bar business and then meeting Marisa for dinner.

"So far, I've narrowed the suspect list to the Naples and Lake Forest, Illinois, telephone directories," I answered her.

"So this case presents a challenge, and that's what interests you," Marisa said. "The old fire-horse-answering-the-bell kind of thing."

A statement, not a question. After a few years of dating, Marisa knew me well.

The next morning, I called Sullivan and said, "I've read the murder book. It's a good start."

"I suggest you begin by getting together with Detective Duncan," he told me. "You can arrange to meet at the Wilberforce house. The murder happened about three weeks ago, so it's not an active crime scene anymore. The hurricane set back our investigation. But I think it would be helpful to check it out anyway."

Henry Wilberforce's house was located on Galleon Drive in Port Royal. Marisa, my real estate expert, told me that Port Royal was one of the most exclusive and pricey neighborhoods in America. She said that, during the 1940s, a retired advertising agency owner named John Glen Sample decided to develop two square miles of mangroves and swamps in Naples by filling in peninsulas of land overlooking canals leading into Naples Bay. Sample gave the streets pirate-themed names like Galleon Drive, Rum Row, and Treasure Lane. He began building small homes, most of which had now been torn down and mansions built in their places. One of those mansions had recently sold for a mind-blowing $48.8 million, a record for Naples, Marisa told me. And then that house was torn down to make way for an even grander one. Unreal. The price I paid for my houseboat wouldn't stock a wine cellar in Port Royal.

I found the Wilberforce house and pulled into the circular driveway. A tan Taurus sedan with a government license plate was there. The house was a two-story yellow stucco with a tile roof and five-car garage. There was no crime-scene tape. Henry already had been buried in the Lake Forest Cemetery, according to the murder book.

I walked along a brick sidewalk to a big brown wooden door, considered ringing the bell, then tried the knob and found it unlocked. I entered a large foyer that resembled the lobby of a Ritz-Carlton. There was a two-story ceiling with a huge crystal chandelier suspended on a gold chain, a curved staircase with an ornate black wrought iron railing leading to the second floor, oil paintings and tapestries on the walls, oriental rugs on the stone floor, a grandfather clock . . . Everything but a suit of armor, which maybe was in the library. It was a place that required a docent to give a proper tour.

Marisa and I had taken an overnight trip to Sarasota to see the Ringling Circus Museum and the Ringling family mansion named Ca' d'Zan. John and Mable Ringling would have felt right at home in Henry Wilberforce's residence.

I found Detective Allie Duncan in the kitchen, seated at a breakfast table with a Starbuck's paper cup, talking on her cell phone. She looked up at me, smiled, and raised her index finger in a just-a-moment gesture. The kitchen was as elaborate as the rest of the house.

She finished her call, smiled, and stood up. Allie Duncan was an African American woman, looking to be in her early thirties, lean and fit, and wearing a navy-blue pants suit and black flats, the shoes being more appropriate for running perps to ground than heels would be. A gold detective shield, just like mine, was clipped to her belt, along with a black leather holster containing a 9mm Beretta.

Huh . . .

An attractive woman with a gun . . .

There was no upside in snapping her photo with my cell phone camera and showing it to Marisa. She would have approved of my Chicago PD partner, a man named Tommy Boyle. Tommy had maybe been lean and fit at birth, but by the time I hooked up with him, he had done his best to desecrate God's Sacred Temple, and succeeded. One time, Tommy had been unable to run down a perp who was in a wheelchair. To be fair, they were going downhill.

Duncan offered her hand, smiled, and said, "I'm Allie Duncan. You're either Jack Starkey or the pool man."

I was wearing my Bruce Springsteen tee shirt so she couldn't be blamed for wondering if I was there to solve a homicide or to test the swimming pool's chlorine balance. I shook her hand and assured her that I was, in fact, Jack Starkey.

"I'd offer you coffee, but I only have the one cup," she said.

"Not a problem, I stopped at a Dunkin' Donuts on the way here."

She walked over to double french doors leading from the kitchen to the back patio. One of the window panes was broken. The crime scene crew must have cleaned up the glass.

"The killer broke this window and unlocked the door," she told me. "No prints on the knob, other than those of Mr. Wilberforce and his staff, his butler and his cook. Let's go up to his bedroom on the second floor. That's where his body was found."

I followed her up the stairs and to the end of a long hallway, past a number of closed doors, which I assumed were guest bedrooms, and into the master bedroom. She walked over to the canopy bed. There were no blankets or sheets, just the mattress, which had a large stain on it. Henry's blood.

"He was found here, in his pajamas, lying under the covers, indicating he was probably asleep when shot," Allie told me. "According to the medical examiner, the .22-caliber bullet shattered upon impact and bounced around in his skull, turning his brain to mush."

Which was why professionals used .22-caliber pistols. They were quiet when fitted with a suppressor, and as deadly up close as larger calibers.

"Who found him?" I asked.

"His butler, Franz Mueller, who lived in an apartment above the garage with his wife, Anna, who was Henry's cook. The couple worked for him here and in his Lake Forest home. They'd been with the Wilberforce family for more than thirty years."

"You spoke with them?"

"Yes," she said. "Franz said he was delivering Henry's morning coffee when he found the body. Neither he nor Anna heard anything during the night. The Muellers went back to Lake Forest."

"The time of death?" I asked.

"The ME puts it sometime between one and four A.M."

Allie looked at the bloodstained mattress, drew in a breath, and asked, "You ever get used to this kind of thing, Jack?"

"If you ever do, it's time to quit," I told her.

She wanted to learn from me, Sullivan said. That was probably the most important thing I had to teach her.

That, and wear your Kevlar vest whenever you were going in harm's way. And that, as a cop, you were always going in harm's way.

We toured the rest of the house and then went out to the backyard: lush grounds landscaped with trees, bushes, and flowers, an outdoor kitchen and fireplace, an Olympic-sized pool, and a cement fountain that was a copy, on a smaller scale, of the Trevi Fountain in Rome. When my then-wife, Claire, and I visited the city on a vacation before our daughter, Jenny, was born, we sought out the fountain because we'd seen it in the movie, *Three Coins in the Fountain*. Showing off, I took off my shoes and socks and waded in, picking up a handful of coins that were Italian, American, and from other countries, and then dropping them back in, lest I be charged with theft by the Carabinieri. Maybe they would have granted a professional courtesy to a Chicago cop and let me off with a scolding. I looked into Henry's fountain as I passed by. No coins.

It was clear from the murder book that the Naples crime scene team had thoroughly processed the house and grounds and found no clues. Still, I liked having a look for myself. I sometimes imagined that the ghosts of murder victims were still present at crime scenes and wanted to tell me who ended their lives. That never happened, but just in case they were watching me, I wanted them to know I was chasing their killers so that their souls could be at rest.

5.

The Eye of the Needle

That afternoon, I stopped by Cubby Cullen's office in the Fort Myers Beach police station to update him. The station was located in a single-story, white concrete-block building on Egret Drive. Cubby's office resembled a man cave, with stuffed game fish on the walls, along with memorabilia of Ohio pro and college sports teams, and a photo of him wearing army camos and a parachute, standing in the open doorway of an airplane, looking back over his shoulder. Presumably that plane would at some point land, so why end the trip prematurely?

"Sounds like just the sort of conundrum you like, Jack," Cubby said as he sat behind his cluttered desk, with me in a chair in front. We both had cups of just-barely drinkable station house coffee. "What's your approach to the case?"

"I'm going to speak with people around town who knew Henry," I answered. "Detective Duncan has already done that, but maybe I'll pick up something she missed. Then, if Sullivan okays the expense, I'll go to Lake Forest and do the same thing there."

I left Cubby's office and drove to The Drunken Parrot, where I had an appointment to meet with someone from a roofing company. It wasn't the first time that the bar's roof had been damaged. A strong wind or heavy rain would do the trick. This time it was damaged by Hurricane Irena. Sam and I had covered it with a blue tarp. There were a lot of blue tarps like that on roofs around town. I wasn't looking forward to the estimate.

"Maybe it's a teardown," Bill said when I called to tell him about the roof. "Good money after bad?"

"Then where would you go to meet college girls during spring break?" I asked.

Without hesitating, he said, "Okay, I'm in for my half."

The cost of repairing the roof was eighteen thousand bucks. I knew the roofer, no need to get a second opinion. When it came to the bar, Bill had his agenda and I had mine, which was to earn some cash, keep myself busy between homicide cases, and, perhaps, as a recovering alcoholic, prove to myself that I had the will power to drink diet root beer in a bar. Think former bank robber owns a bank. So far, I had the will power, but the recovery rule was one day at a time. In addition, I always enjoyed the warm conviviality of bars, and still did, even without the alcoholic haze.

You can't change the past or be certain about the future. Today is the only canvas on which to paint the portrait of your life. Brother Timothy at Loyola told us that. He was one of the good clerics. He thought hard about resigning from the priesthood when the sexual abuse scandal first broke, he told me, but decided to stay within the church and try to persuade any abusers he came across that they needed to see the error of their ways. He said that, as a seminarian, he'd heard rumors about the abuse, and would forever wish he'd followed up on them, but the internal culture was don't ask, don't tell. So who was he to judge others? He'd been a professional boxer before becoming a priest, a ranked middleweight, so I knew he could be very persuasive. Let's just say that my friends and I were never late for class when we were his students. And maybe an abuser or two finally, at Brother Timothy's urging, did get true religion.

Father Benson Hargrove was the priest of Trinity-by-the-Cove Episcopal Church on Galleon Drive in Port Royal. You could walk there from the Wilberforce house, which, I learned, Henry often did. It was the only church in the neighborhood, and was built by John Glen Sample, the Port Royal developer.

We were seated in comfortable leather club chairs near a stained-glass window in Father Hargrove's study. The pattern in the stained-glass window depicted Christ on the Cross. Father Hargrove had been preparing his Sunday sermon when I arrived, he told me. Perhaps the topic was "Maybe a Camel *Can* Pass Through the Eye of a Needle." Jesus said it is easier for a camel to pass through the eye of a needle than for a rich person to enter the kingdom of God. As I observed during my first Naples murder investigation, if Jesus was right, then why should the residents of Port Royal contribute to the church's building fund and stuff the collection plate with big bucks if it wasn't going to gain them entry to the heavenly kingdom? It was Father Hargrove's job to reassure his flock that their generosity provided a loophole. By that measure, when they got to heaven, they'd find Henry Wilberforce there.

Hanging on the wall near Father Hargrove's desk were diplomas from Dartmouth College and the Yale Divinity School. Ivy League all the way. I'd always imagined that the Episcopal Church was for the white-collar class. Nothing wrong with that, except for that eye-of-the-needle problem.

"We had a very nice memorial service for Henry before he was flown home to Lake Forest," Father Hargrove told me. "He was a fine man and a real friend of the church."

"I've heard he had good days and bad days, mentally speaking," I said.

"That's true. In that regard, he was no different from a great many of our parishioners. Except that no one else ever came to Sunday services wearing a Chicago Cubs uniform."

Marisa had told me that, because of the advanced age of many Naples residents, there were as many churches in Naples as golf courses, filled with sinners seeking last-minute absolution.

"What about money?" I asked. "I've heard that Henry was quite a philanthropist."

"He was very generous with his tithes," Father Hargrove said. "He knew that our church needed a new roof, that the furnace was about to give up the ghost, and that the plumbing had to have its lead pipes replaced by copper. He asked me what all that would cost. The next Sunday, he put a check for the full amount in the collection plate."

I wished that Henry had walked into The Drunken Parrot after the hurricane: *Drinks on the house, my good man, and let me tell you about our roof problem.*

"Are there many home invasions in Port Royal?" I asked, playing along with the cover story.

"No, thankfully, there are not. The Naples Police Department is very good about patrolling the streets, and the Port Royal Neighborhood Watch program is very active."

The housekeeper reappeared with coffee and pastries. Bless her heart. She'd have no trouble passing through the eye of the needle.

Father Hargrove winked and said. "Don't quote me on this, Detective Starkey, but it's such a shame that the burglar chose Henry's house. Just between you, me, and the Virgin Mary, not all Port Royal residents are as generous as he was."

The bad guy had killed the reverend's golden goose.

Next on my interview list was Leila Purcell, chairwoman of the board of the Miriam Wilberforce Art Museum. I read on the museum's website that it had been called the Naples Museum of Art until a year ago, when Henry donated a number of paintings from his personal art collection, including works by Picasso, Matisse, Rembrandt, Gustav Klimt, and Edward Hopper.

I wasn't an art expert, but Claire was into that stuff, sometimes dragging me to museums and lectures in Chicago, so I recognized the names of the artists of the paintings Henry had donated to the museum, and I was certain that they were worth megabucks. My trade-off for going to the museums and lectures with Claire was that she would go to Cubs games with me, followed by drinks at The Baby Doll Polka Lounge. Actually, I think she kind of liked doing that, although she never admitted it.

At Leila's suggestion, I met her for lunch at Olde Naples Country Club. It was, as Yogi Berra said, "*Déjà vu* all over again." Which was also the title of John Fogerty's sixth solo studio album. I dined at Olde Naples CC during my first Naples murder case with a fine woman named Ashley Howe who was instrumental in helping me solve the murders.

Leila Purcell was of an age when pretty women were called "handsome." She had short, stylishly cut silver hair, and was wearing a white pants suit with pink trim and a pearl necklace with matching earrings. I again was wearing my preppie uniform. For all anyone knew, I'd graduated from Yale and the Harvard Business School instead of from Loyola and the Chicago Police Academy. Until, perhaps, I spoke.

When I arrived, Leila was seated at a table near the windows overlooking the golf course, sipping a glass of white wine. Back in my drinking days, the only wine I consumed was Cold Duck. I once told Marisa that and she was genuinely horrified.

Leila put her purse from the table onto one of the unoccupied chairs as I sat opposite her, shook her head, and said, "Kate Spade. Such a shame."

I had no idea who she was talking about, but I didn't ask so as to hide my ignorance. Was a woman named Kate Spade supposed to join us, but something had prevented her from doing so?

"Thank you for seeing me," I told Leila as a white-jacketed waiter brought the menus and took our drink orders, an Arnie Palmer for me and another white wine for her.

"Henry Wilberforce was a saint," she said. "Whoever killed him should be castrated."

An observation that made me like her a lot.

"I assume you don't know why a burglar would target his house," I said, again sticking to the Naples PD party line.

"No idea whatsoever," she answered.

I knew she didn't, of course. but I was trying, with these interviews, to get a sense of Henry Wilberforce the man, and to see where that led, if anywhere. Why did a man who, everyone said, had no enemies, have at least one?

"What were the circumstances of Henry's gift of those paintings to the museum?" I asked Leila.

"No different from other gifts we've received, I'd say."

"I mean, was he . . . lucid?"

"Define lucid," she said.

"Did Henry fully understand the magnitude of his gift, would you say?"

"One afternoon Henry was in the museum," Leila said. "He asked a docent if I was there. I knew Henry and Miriam well, you see. I wasn't there, but the docent, a woman named Tamara Cox, not that it matters what her name was, called me at home, and I came right over. I found Henry in the Modern Art Gallery, looking at an Andy Warhol. I forget which one, but that doesn't matter either, does it? It might have been his painting of a Campbell's tomato soup can, or the one of Marilyn Monroe, which is my favorite—not, as I said, that it matters to your investigation. Henry asked me if I thought that the Warhol painting, whichever one it was, was worthy of hanging in the museum. I said, yes, I did. He said he really didn't much like modern art, and that he had a few paintings he thought the museum might want. A few days later, I got a call from his lawyer in Lake Forest, whose name I can't recall at the moment, not that it matters, and, a week later, it was a Tuesday, I think, or maybe a Wednesday, whichever, a truck arrived at the museum with the paintings, which had been in his Lake Forest home. Or maybe his home was in Lake Bluff, not that . . ."

"What is the value of the paintings?" I asked her, cutting her off in mid *not that*.

"Priceless, I'd say."

"Did you talk with him about anything else at the museum that day?" I asked her.

She said: "Oh, just idle chitchat. He was wearing a Civil War uniform, Union Army, I think it was, not that it matters which side of the war his uniform represented. It was blue, so Union Army, now that I think of it. An officer's uniform, I think, although I don't recall which rank, not that I'd know a lieutenant from a general. My late husband, Chester, was a colonel in the army when he retired, so if Henry was a colonel, I might have recognized that insignia. Not that it matters, as I said. Fortunately, we didn't have to live on Chester's army pay because my parents were quite wealthy, you see. But of course you don't care about that, Detective Starkey. Anyway, Henry sometimes wore all sorts of costumes, I don't recall what other kinds at the moment, but that's of no consequence to our discussion, so I didn't find the fact that he was dressed that way to be unusual or worth mentioning to him."

Leila's manner of discourse gave new meaning to the word rambling. I never knew where an interview was going to lead, but the odds were that this one was leading me to slit my wrists with a butter knife. Or hers.

The waiter returned and we gave him our lunch orders. We talked more about what a fine man Henry was, a conversation laced with Leila's many digressions. When lunch was finished, I thanked her for her time and offered to pay the check, knowing that I'd be reimbursed by the Naples PD. She looked at me as if trying to understand what I meant, and then said, "Oh, no, that won't be necessary. Guests aren't allowed to pay for anything at the club."

Well, *excuuuuse me.*

Driving home, I thought: Here was another example of Henry Wilberforce behaving oddly and giving away lots of money and expensive gifts, in an apparently unplanned way. Maybe that had something to do with his murder, and maybe it did not. My investigation was still in the "maybe" stage. Sometimes, investigations remained there in perpetuity.

It went like that with other beneficiaries of Henry Wilberforce's largesse: the head of the local humane society, which now could afford to be a no-kill shelter; the Naples Players, an amateur theater company, moving to a new, larger building; the Boys and Girls Club, which could now offer the kids hot meals after school; the Naples Municipal Golf Course, which now gave free lessons to junior players; the Naples Public Library, which now had Henry's collection of first-edition classics. And more.

Henry was missed, everyone said. No one had any idea about why his house was targeted by a homicidal burglar. If Henry turned down the wrong person looking for a handout, a person with a screw loose, that could be a motive for his murder. It would have to be someone capable of murder, and highly skilled. Not many people were both. Whenever you came across people like that, you locked them up.

↺

TOM SULLIVAN had given me the name of Henry's lawyer in Lake Forest. Having learned all I could in Naples, I needed to call him to make an appointment to meet with him. I went to The Drunken Parrot, had a burger while sitting at the bar, then made myself comfortable in my favorite booth and called the lawyer, Brandon Taylor. When he answered, I introduced myself and told him that I was investigating the murder of his client.

"I already spoke with another Naples detective," Taylor said. "But I'm happy to speak with you as well."

He agreed to see me in his office the next day.

6.

My Kind of Town

I sold my Wrigleyville duplex when I moved to Florida. Renting the duplex's second apartment had provided a nice income to supplement my detective's salary and the money I got from Bill Stevens's books. Whenever a tenant couldn't pay the rent, I let it slide. "Do unto others as you would have them do unto you," Jesus said in the Sermon on the Mount. However, when one tenant was eight months behind in his rent, and didn't seem inclined to ever pay up, even though it was clear he had the cash because he bought a new Camaro, I was forced to do unto him what I wouldn't want to have done unto me. When he moved in, he didn't know I was a cop. When he moved out, he did.

Some of my colleagues on the police force didn't need an additional income because one of the benefits of police work in Chicago included the availability of payoffs to look the other way. I had many opportunities for that, but my family upbringing and Jesuit education prevented me from even considering it. However, I did commit sins of omission by not ratting out the crooked cops. I stayed in touch with Brother Timothy after I graduated from Loyola. When I talked to him about the situation, he said he understood that by reporting the corruption, I would compromise my effectiveness as a police officer, and might even "accidentally" get shot by another policeman during a gunfight or have a call for help go unanswered. It had happened. "Life is a balancing act,"

Brother Timothy told me. "You do your best to not fall on your ass."

Bill Stevens had a guest room in the apartment building he owned that I used whenever in town. I kept a toothbrush there. I flew from Fort Myers airport to O'Hare on a Thursday morning: a sunny eighty-four degrees when I left, an overcast twenty-nine degrees, snow on the ground, when I arrived. I took a brown leather bomber jacket from my overnight bag and slipped it on before exiting the terminal. The Hawk, which is what jazz singer Lou Rawls called the frigid wind blowing in off Lake Michigan, hit me head on. I didn't mind. Perfect weather can get boring. A little adversity adds spice to the stew.

Speaking of stew, it was lunchtime, so I took a taxi to The Baby Doll Polka Lounge. You couldn't get an authentic Italian beef sandwich with sweet peppers, dipped in savory beef juice, in Fort Myers Beach. My short-order cook at The Drunken Parrot, a woman named Alice Radinsky, who was a former Marine Corps mess sergeant, gave up when I kept rejecting her attempts to duplicate the sandwich, so it wasn't on our menu. When I inadvertently made a sour face when biting into her latest attempt, she said, "Well then fuck it and the horse it rode in on." I didn't think "it" meant the sandwich.

The Baby Doll was a neighborhood joint in the best sense of that word, a hangout for cops, firemen, pols, print journalists, and whoever else the wind blew in. Too low-rent for the broadcast people who preferred to dine on white tablecloths in places where they'd be recognized and fawned over. Once a guy with luck as bad as it got tried to stick up The Baby Doll. He might as well have tried to rob the police department's shooting range.

"Well, as I live and breathe, it's Jack Starkey," Lucille, the veteran bartender, said as I arrived. "I was beginning to think it was something I said."

I slid onto a barstool and said, "I moved to Florida five years ago, Lucille."

"Huh," she said. "I only recently noticed your absence. Your usual still your usual?"

"Good to see you too, Lucille. Yeah, my usual."

She served me a mug of Berghoff diet root beer, another Chicago specialty which they had on tap, and shouted toward the kitchen door, "One beef, wet, with sweet peppers, no onions, and put wheels on it!"

No need for an intercom at The Baby Doll.

As I waited for my food, I felt a hand on my shoulder and turned to see Dominick Bevilaqua, a detective in the vice unit. He'd always been teased about his last name because it was the same as one of the hoods in *The Sopranos* TV series.

"You're under arrest for exposing yourself on the L," Dom told me. "The security cameras couldn't see your face, but your little limp dick was clearly visible. A dead giveaway."

I said, "Hey, Dom, buy you a beer?"

"Does Oprah like shrimp and grits?" he said as he took the stool next to mine.

Dom had been through the department's required sensitivity training course and flunked it.

Lucille spotted him, drew a frosty mug of Goose Island Pilsner, a beer that was made not five miles from where we were sitting, and slid it down the bar top to him without spilling any. When it came to tending bar, Lucille had mad skills.

"You still living down in the tropics, Jack?" he asked me.

"Fort Myers Beach, in Florida," I answered as my sandwich arrived. Dom stared at it, so I asked Lucille for a knife and another plate and gave him half.

"Whataya doin' these days?" he asked as he took a bite of the sandwich. The juice dripped down his chin and onto his tie, just like it's supposed to.

"I own a bar," I answered.

"Ironic, isn't it? For a . . ."

"Recovering alcoholic. I make it work."

"We're havin' a retirement party here tomorrow night for Johnny McBride," he told me. "You oughta come and see everyone." "I will if I can, Dom," I said. "That'd be nice."

I knew I wouldn't because there was nothing more boring than hearing inebriated cops tell war stories. I used to do plenty of that during my drinking days. Dom and I chatted a while longer, and I greeted other old pals who came in. Then I picked up my overnight bag and caught the L to Wrigleyville, smiling at the security cameras and pointing at my crotch for Dom's benefit.

I walked to Bill Stevens's apartment building from the L station and took the elevator up to his eighth-floor apartment. I knew he'd be at work at the *Chicago Tribune*, but I had a key. The building was one of those known as Wrigleyville Rooftops, which were vintage mid-rise apartment buildings on Waveland and Sheffield Avenues near Wrigley Field whose flat roofs provided clear views of Cubs games. Because of that, they were valuable and didn't turn over often. I put my bag in the guest room and went to the kitchen to brew a pot of coffee.

I had an hour before I needed to catch the commuter train to Lake Forest. I'd brought the manuscript of *Stoney's Downfall* and used the time to continue my editing. I knew Bill would ask about my progress when I saw him the next morning. He was in Milwaukee on a story and would be home late.

My train car was packed with commuters, like sardines in a can, going home from jobs in the city to stops along the North Shore of Lake Michigan: Evanston, Wilmette, Kenilworth, Winnetka, Glencoe, Highland Park, Highwood, Fort Sheridan, Lake Forest, and Lake Bluff. If you stayed on the train, you'd get to North Chicago, Waukegan, Kenosha, Wisconsin, and other towns generally considered too distant for the commute to Chicago, and finally to Milwaukee. One good reason to go to Milwaukee was the bratwurst-and-sauerkraut sandwich at Miller Park, home of the

Brewers. If there was another good reason to go to Milwaukee, I couldn't come up with it. Then again, I was from Chicago.

It was a one-hour train ride from downtown Chicago to Lake Forest, a city that, beginning with the arrival of the railroad in 1855, became a summer retreat for wealthy Chicago families. I recalled reading a story in the *Chicago Tribune* saying that Macy's, the big New York department store company that acquired Marshall Field's, a Chicago institution, much to the consternation of Chicagoans, was closing its little store in Lake Forest. It had been opened in 1928 by Marshall Field III, grandson of the founder, because he wanted his wife to have a place to shop when in residence at their summer home.

My ex-wife, Claire, found that to be an "absolutely charming gift from a husband to his wife," and she suggested that I should see if the Chicago PD would open a precinct station near our house in Lincoln Park in case she needed police assistance at a moment's notice, and I wasn't available. I told her I'd put that into the department's suggestion box, which was a wastebasket.

I disembarked, along with a group of Lake Forest residents, at the Downtown Lake Forest Station, there being another stop on the city's west side.

The office of Brandon Taylor Esq, attorney-at-law, was right across the street from the train station, in Market Square. I found a brass plaque with his name on it next to a doorway leading to the second floor of a white stucco building, with a Williams Sonoma store on the street level. Kitchen appliances were on display in the store window. I'd be hard pressed to know what any one of them did. I once bought an electric can opener for Joe's food but couldn't get the thing to let go of the can, so I tossed it.

I walked up the stairs, entered an office through a pebbled-glass door with Brandon Taylor's name on it, and stepped into a reception area with no receptionist. The door chimed when I opened it and Taylor came out through a door to greet me. He looked to be in his mid-thirties.

"Mr. Starkey?" he said. "I'm Brandon Taylor. Let's go to my office and chat."

There was only one office, indicating that he was a solo practitioner.

"How long have you represented Henry Wilberforce?" I asked when we were seated in club chairs by the office window.

"For the last six years," he said. "Before that, my father handled his personal legal affairs, and before that, my grandfather represented Henry's father."

"As I said on the phone, I'm here because the circumstances of your client's death, at first thought by the police to be the result of a burglary gone wrong, now indicate he'd been targeted for murder," I told him. "Do you have any idea about who might have done that?"

"I'll tell you what I told that other Naples detective when she called. I have no idea who might have murdered Henry, or why," he answered. "Everyone who knew Henry liked him. His father and his grandfather, who built Wilberforce Foods into a multibillion-dollar business, were hard men who made enemies along the way. Henry worked for the company, eventually becoming chairman of the board and chief executive officer, but he wasn't like that."

"Does he have any living family?" I asked. "I know that his wife and son are deceased."

"Henry was an only child," Taylor said. "There are two nieces and a nephew on his wife Miriam's side of the family, the children of her brother and sisters. As far as I know, Henry hadn't seen them in many years."

"Are they his heirs?"

"No. They each inherited five-hundred thousand from their Aunt Miriam. They probably assumed they were in their Uncle Henry's will, too, for some substantial amount. If they know he's dead, they now also know they won't inherit anything because I haven't contacted them. Henry's entire estate was left to his charitable foundation, other than his house here, and its contents, which he donated to the Lake Forest Historical Society. I think they intend to make it a museum."

"I'm wondering if Henry's killer was someone who asked him for money and was turned down," I said.

"That's possible," Taylor answered. "But I have no way to identify such a person. In recent years, Henry's gifts outside his foundation were random. He told me where to transfer money or to send a check or to have some item delivered, but not the identity of anyone he might have refused, if, in fact, he ever refused anyone."

"What about his butler and cook, Franz and Anna Mueller?"

"Henry provided for them generously in his will. They helped me gather up his personal effects from the house, which I have in a storage locker, and then they returned to their native Austria," he said.

"Detective Duncan interviewed the Muellers in Naples," I told him. "She said she had no reason to suspect them."

"I agree," Taylor said. "They were like family to him."

"Did you examine his personal effects?"

"Yes, of course. I found nothing that I thought related to his murder."

"I'd like to look at them too," I said.

"Not a problem," Taylor told me.

At my request, Taylor made appointments for me with the Lake Forest mayor, police chief, and several other people who knew Henry well over the years. He drove me to meet with them in his BMW 750iL, a sweet ride if you could pay the freight. All of those people told the same story as Taylor and everyone in Naples: Henry Wilberforce was a kind and generous man who had no enemies. Many of the people I interviewed asked me why I was doing such a thorough investigation for a home invasion that had inadvertently resulted in Henry's death, as had been reported in the news media. I told them what I'd told Brandon Taylor, that it now appeared to be a murder, which shocked them. Just like everyone else who knew Henry, these people could not imagine why anyone would want to kill him. A man who owned a house next door to

Henry's said, unkindly I thought, "Murdering a man his age seems a bit, uh, redundant, doesn't it, Detective?"

Then we drove to Taylor's storage locker where I spent nearly an hour going through boxes of Henry's files and other personal items. I found nothing that might help my investigation. However, there were boxes of old mint-condition baseball cards. I opened one of the boxes and selected a card at random. It was a Honus Wagner. The Flying Dutchman. I knew that another Honus Wagner card sold at auction a few years ago for $2.1 million. "Henry started the collection as a boy," Taylor told me. "I've got an appraiser coming. The value will be in the millions."

"Is Henry buried near here?" I asked Taylor when I was finished.

"Yes," he told me. "In Lake Forest Cemetery, with Miriam and Peter."

"I'd like to go there," I said.

My old feeling that the dead wanted to tell me what happened to them.

The cemetery was at the end of Lake Street. We drove through large wrought iron gates and then along a winding asphalt road lined with oak trees. Taylor parked and we got out of the car. He pointed toward one of the trees and said, "Right over that way."

I followed him to the site of three graves with granite markers bearing the names and dates of birth and death of Henry Wilberforce, Miriam Wilberforce, and Peter Wilberforce.

I looked down at Henry's grave and silently asked him who his killer was. He told me, a whisper on the wind, that it was my job to find out, as they all did.

"We can go now," I told Taylor.

He drove me to the station and I took the train back to Chicago. I'd arranged to have dinner with Claire and our daughter, Jenny, that night. Claire was now married to an orthopedic surgeon, several steps up from the alcoholic homicide detective she'd first been married to, and Jenny was married to an assistant US attorney.

I had an hour before our reservation at Spiaggia, an Italian restaurant in the atrium of the One Mag Mile Building on Michigan Avenue, a favorite of mine and Claire's back in the day. I caught a taxi from Union Station to Graceland Cemetery on North Clark Street, my second cemetery of the day, but this time I wasn't working. I told the driver to turn in through the front gates. Graceland was the final resting place of many prominent Chicagoans, but I didn't care about any of them, except to note that two of the inhabitants were Alan Pinkerton, founder of the famous detective agency, and Kate Warne, his employee and the first female detective in the United States.

I had the driver follow the road to the gravesites of my father, mother, and brother, and asked him to wait. I got out of the cab, turned up the collar of my jacket against the wind, and walked over; there was a fourth plot, reserved for me. I lived in Fort Myers Beach, but Chicago would always be home.

Then I did what I always did when visiting there. I updated my father on the Cubs prospects for next season, told my mother how much I missed her and her cooking, and told my brother about my current investigation. Whenever I visited, their presence was palpable, and comforting. A Starkey family reunion is how I thought of it.

Then I got back into the taxi and gave the driver the address of Bill's apartment building.

Back at the apartment, I called Marisa.

"Have you learned anything of value?" she asked me.

"Just that I need to find a person who wanted something from Henry Wilberforce and didn't get it."

"Needle in a haystack," she said.

"Needle in the Milky Way."

"The galaxy or the candy bar?"

While I pondered that question, Marisa asked when I was coming home. It would have been beyond rude to tell her that I was home, so I said I had a flight the next morning.

I got to Spiaggia early and was at the window table where Claire and I always sat. It had a panoramic view of Lake Michigan over the Oak Street Beach. After ten minutes, I spotted my girls being led to my table by a waiter in a tuxedo. They both looked terrific, turning heads in their wake. The last time I was in Chicago, five months earlier, to attend the funeral of a retired cop friend who'd died of cirrhosis of the liver, Claire was at a charity ball with Doctor Quack and Jenny was away on a business trip, so I hadn't seen them in a while.

The time before that was during the Christmas holiday. I was invited to Christmas dinner at Claire's house, a Victorian in the city's Gold Coast neighborhood. I got there early to exchange gifts with Claire and Jenny. The husbands weren't part of that deal; they retreated to the family room, no doubt to discuss what an outstanding ex-husband and father I was, while the three of us sat in the living room by the Christmas tree, logs crackling and sparking in the fireplace.

Claire thoughtfully gave me a leather-bound set of Arthur Conan Doyle's four Sherlock Holmes novels; I'd only read one of them. Jenny gave me a garish tie featuring a palm tree and a woman in a hula skirt as a joke, and a wood-framed photo of my Chicago Police Academy class, which her husband, Brad Thornhill, an assistant US attorney in Chicago, somehow obtained, and which I loved.

I'd asked Santa for a Dan Wesson 1911 .45-caliber semiautomatic pistol with a pearl grip, but he must have put it in someone else's stocking by mistake. A pity, because those babies went for north of sixteen hundred bucks, if you got the 4.25-inch barrel.

Marisa picked out a Hermes scarf featuring a jaguar for Claire, and, for Jenny, something called a cashmere pashmina. They kindly maintained the ruse that I'd done the shopping and, with a wink at one another, complimented my excellent taste in ladies' fashion.

I'd never before met Claire's second husband, Dr. Evan McMaster, the orthopedic surgeon. I was disappointed to find that he was a thoroughly fine fellow. I discovered via Google that he was one of the best at his trade in the country, that he'd developed a new technique for hip replacements now widely used by the profession, that he'd been an All-America squash player at the University of Pennsylvania, and first in his class at the Johns Hopkins University School of Medicine. If I'd been any one of those things, Evan would have heard about it before I asked him to pass the gravy. I did earn some medals in the marines, and as a cop, and considered wearing them on my sweater to the dinner, but I decided that would be too showy.

When Claire and Jenny reached my table, I stood and kissed them both on the cheek.

"You still clean up nicely, Jack," Claire said, smiling, as they took their seats. For that occasion, I'd packed a grey suit.

"How are you, Dad?" Jenny asked.

"As good as can be expected, given what I have to work with," I answered, and we both laughed. It was our running joke, dating back to her girlhood.

She put her hand on my arm. "Seriously."

"I'm good, honey. Keeping busy with the bar, and the occasional homicide investigation. That's why I'm here."

"Tell us about it," Claire said.

When we were married, I never discussed my cases with Claire. The idea was to leave my work at the office. I talked to a bottle of Jack Daniel's Black instead.

The waiter arrived and took drink orders, chardonnay for Claire, pinot grigio for Jenny, and club soda with lime for me. Then I told them about my case.

"I know who Henry Wilberforce was, of course, and I read about his death in the *Tribune*," Claire said. "In fact, I wondered if you'd be on that investigation, because he died in Naples, and you helped the police there once before."

"Be careful, Dad," Jenny said. "Given what happened during your last two Florida cases."

"I'm wearing my Kevlar vest right now," I said. When they didn't smile, I added, "Kidding."

The waiter took our dinner orders and we chatted amiably while we ate. At one point, Claire asked, "Are you still seeing that . . ."

"Realtor," I answered. "Yes."

Maybe she meant to say "floozie." But Claire wasn't like that. I wanted to ask her if she was still married to that second-rate sawbones. I was like that, but I didn't.

"Is it serious?" Jenny asked.

She knew I still loved her mother. She wanted me to move on and be happy. As did Claire.

"Serious is as serious does," I answered enigmatically, and Jenny let it go.

I will never forgive myself for blowing it with my family. I once asked Brother Timothy if I ever could, and he said, no, probably not, only God could. "The forgiveness business is hard, but fair," he said. He also said, "I learned a lesson as a boxer, Jack. It doesn't matter how many times you get knocked down, it only matters how many times you get up, and the two numbers need to be the same."

Amen to that.

The next morning, before flying home, Bill and I walked to Lou Mitchell's, a restaurant on West Jackson Boulevard near Union Station that had been serving great breakfasts and lunches since 1923. Lou's was one of those places luminaries frequented: politicians, movie stars, rock stars, business leaders, famous authors, and important clerics. It was said that a Pope once stopped in for pancakes.

We sat at the counter, as we always did. I ordered a belgian malted pecan waffle. Bill got a Greek sausage omelet.

"So how's the book editing going?" Bill asked while we waited for our food.

"I'm on it," I said. "But sometimes, real murders get in the way."

"Light a fire under it," he said. "The deadline's almost here."

Bill waved at a man at a nearby table, who I knew to be his city editor, then said, "You told me you're here on a case."

"You know about what happened to Henry Wilberforce," I said.

"Sure. It was in all the papers, including mine."

"Off the record?"

"Always," he assured me.

"It wasn't a home invasion gone bad, it was a targeted murder," I told him.

He gave a low whistle and said, "At some future time, that'd make a great plot for a Jack Stoney book. He'll solve the case, of course. With you, we'll see."

7.

No Stone Unturned

Sometimes, when stumped by a difficult case, it helped me to let the facts churn around in my subconscious brain. I did that, for a week, busying myself with business at the bar, helping Marisa plant some kind of flowers in her backyard, a task I ranked the same as attending an art lecture, and disciplining myself to exercise by running and doing sit-ups and push-ups, a regimen I'd let slide.

One morning, I was running along the beach, taking note of the passing scene, including people who looked good in skimpy bathing suits and people who did not. Among the latter group were old, fat men who wore tiny, tight bikini bottoms showing off their packages, which identified them as other than American, in my experience. Marisa said she thought that those bulges were rolled-up socks.

When I finished my run and was walking to cool down, like a racehorse after exercise, an idea did find its way from my subconscious to conscious mind: Brandon Taylor, Henry's lawyer, mentioned that Henry had a nephew and two nieces. Even though they hadn't been in touch with their uncle in years, and weren't in his will, I decided it would be worthwhile to speak with them.

When I got home from the beach, I called Brandon Taylor and found out that the nephew, Nelson Lowry, lived in Santa Monica, California; one niece, June Dumont, lived in Washington, DC; and the other niece, Libby Leverton, resided in Boston. Taylor gave me their phone numbers and addresses.

Using my cell phone to connect with my sleuthing partner Google as I sat in my regular booth at The Drunken Parrot, I found newspaper articles in the *Santa Monica Mirror* and the *Los Angeles Times* reporting that Nelson "Scooter" Lowry won a lot of sailboat races, was an alternate on an American boat for an America's Cup race six years ago, was named one of Santa Monica's "Most Eligible Bachelors" eight years ago, had twice been arrested for drunk driving, and had partnered with two other men in starting a vineyard in the Napa Valley which, before it could produce any wine, burned up in a wildfire. There was no mention of Scooter having a job, other than the failed vineyard investment. I found an obituary for his father, Langdon Lowry, who had been a Silicon Valley venture capitalist, indicating that Scooter was a trust-funder. Good for him. I wouldn't have turned down a nice, cozy trust fund.

I called Scooter and left a voice mail, explaining who I was, why I wanted to speak with him, and that his Uncle Henry's lawyer had given me his name.

He called back the next day, saying that he'd just come back from the Baja 1000 race, held on the Baja California Peninsula. It was a race in which cars, trucks, motorcycles, ATVs, and dune buggies competed, he told me.

"How'd you do?" I asked him.

"Dumped my Suzuki an hour in," he answered.

"Bad luck," I told him. "As I said in my voice mail, I'd like to talk to you about your uncle, Henry Wilberforce. Your late uncle, I should say."

After a pause, Scooter said, "My late uncle? You mean he died?"

"Yes, he did."

"Well, Uncle Henry was in his eighties. He had a long and happy life."

"Right up until the moment that someone shot him in the head in his home in Naples, Florida."

"What? That's awful!" Scooter said, sounding truly shocked. "Did you catch the person who did it?"

"Not yet."

"Is there a motive?"

"I don't know yet," I said, adding, "Your uncle was a very generous person."

"Uncle Henry's and Aunt Miriam's charity did a lot of good work," he said. "Clean drinking water for Africa, AIDs research, arts grants . . . I read a story about that in the *LA Times* some years ago."

I wondered if he knew that Henry's giving had gone far beyond the foundation's. I decided not to tell him that yet in case he did know it and wasn't telling me, which could be an indication of his guilt. Or not.

"When was the last time you saw your uncle?" I asked him.

"Hhmmm . . . A long time ago. I can't remember when. I wasn't able to attend Aunt Miriam's funeral, so it was before then."

He was probably in a sailboat or motorcycle race at the time of his aunt's funeral, or maybe he had a hot dinner date. But he had the time to cash his check for the five-hundred K. Never too busy for a trip to the bank.

"Thanks, Scooter," I said. "This has been helpful."

"Okay," he said. "Let me know if you need anything else."

"I will. I may have to talk to you again," I said.

"Let me ask a favor," he said. "Can you tell the lawyer that I'm available to help with any of Uncle Henry's affairs, me being a relative and all?"

Meaning: Just in case I'm in his will.

"I'll do that," I promised.

"Okay then, Detective Starkey," he said. "I'll let you go."

When someone ended a phone call by telling me they'd let me go, it always seemed like they were firing me. Just a minor annoyance on the scale of things. I concluded that either Scooter did not know his uncle was dead until I told him, and therefore was innocent of the crime, or that he was a very good actor.

Next up was June Dumont in our nation's capital. It was clear from online newspaper and magazine articles that her husband, Alan, was one of Washington's most powerful and successful lawyers. His law firm, Chesney, Hartson, Dumont & Hamilton, also had offices in New York, Los Angeles, and London. The partners shuffled back and forth between the firm and top jobs in Republican presidential administrations. One senior partner had been secretary of state, another ambassador to the Court of Saint James, and another US attorney general. June Dumont was active in the city's social scene, and she served on the boards of a number of charitable institutions. All the right ones, I was certain.

I could picture the Dumonts at White House state dinners and opening their home for GOP fundraising events. Their house was in Sheridan-Kalorama, one of Washington's highest-end neighborhoods, my online research told me. The French ambassador lived on one side of their house and a Supreme Court justice on the other, an article in *Washingtonian Magazine* said. The Dumont house was once owned by Woodrow Wilson, according to that article. Barack and Michelle Obama lived nearby. I wondered if Alan, Barack, the French ambassador, and the Supreme Court justice had a regular poker night or got together to watch football games and down a few brewskis. That's what my pals and I did in Wrigleyville.

I called the Dumonts' home number and got no answer and no prompt to leave a voice mail. Then I looked up the number for Alan's law firm.

"Good morning, Chesney, Hartson, Dumont & Hamilton," the receptionist said. "How may I help you?"

By the time she got to the question after saying the name of the firm, I'd almost forgotten why I called.

"This is Detective Jack Starkey," I said. "I'd like to speak to Alan Dumont."

"May I ask what this is regarding?"

"You may," I assured her. "It is regarding a death."

"Oh my," she said.

"Not to worry, it's no one you know," I assured her.

"One moment please," she said. "I'll put you on hold and see if Mr. Dumont is available."

The on-hold music was John Coltrane blowing a jazz riff on his tenor sax. Points for that.

"This is Alan Dumont," a voice said after I'd listened to Coltrane for around five minutes. I could have held on much longer. "Now what's this about a death?"

Alan sounded extremely annoyed. I was taking him away from whatever job he was over-billing a zillion dollars an hour to.

"Your wife's uncle, Henry Wilberforce, died in his home in Naples, Florida," I told him, hoping he wouldn't bill me for the conversation. "I'd like to speak with June about that. There was no answer at your home."

"June hasn't been in touch with Henry for many years," Alan said. "I'm certain she doesn't know he died. I can tell her about that, so you don't need to."

"I'm interviewing all of Mr. Wilberforce's friends and relatives," I said. "I have a few questions about the way he died."

"June is very busy," he said. "She has no time for you today."

Probably busy with her Pilates class or shopping at Cartier or having a ladies' lunch. A killer schedule.

"I'd appreciate it if you'd have her call me when she's available," I said.

"I'll do that, Detective," Alan Dumont said.

He hung up without asking for my phone number. No matter, June Dumont wouldn't be calling me anyway.

Then I called Libby Leverton in Boston. She answered on the fourth ring. I told her who I was and why I was calling.

"Oh . . . my . . . I didn't know that Uncle Henry was dead," she said.

Maybe she really didn't know, or maybe she and Scooter had studied with the same acting coach.

"When is the last time you saw or spoke with Henry?" I asked her.

"Let me think . . . I must have last seen my uncle at Aunt Miriam's funeral in Lake Forest. That was about ten years ago. Not since then."

I decided I could get nothing more from that call, so I said, "I might have to speak with you again." I said that to everybody during an investigation, whether I needed to or not. Kept them on the hook.

"Yes, that would be fine," she said, and we ended the call without her telling me that she was letting me go.

I needed to digest my conversations with Scooter and Libby and to figure out how to connect with June. But first I needed to digest a cheeseburger for lunch. A burger contained all the important food groups, as long as you didn't consider vitamins, minerals, and fiber to be important food groups.

That night, over drinks at my bar, I gave Marisa an update on my investigation.

"Is one of them a more likely suspect than the other?" she asked me.

"I still need to connect with June Dumont. At this point, I'd pick the nephew, Scooter Lowry. He comes from a wealthy family, but he seems to be a slacker. Maybe his family cut him off, or he spent all his money on drugs, or gambling, or fast women. June's husband is a partner in a hotshot law firm, so probably not her. The other niece, Libby Leverton, is married to a big real estate developer in Boston. So probably not her either. I'm hoping that self-preservation is kicking in and that they're not talking to each other about my investigation, each of them hoping to point me at one of the others."

"Fast women?" Marisa said, an eyebrow raised. I knew that phrase was a mistake as soon as I said it. "Isn't that a chauvinistic, anachronistic, sexist concept?"

"I was just thinking like Scooter would," I explained.

"Close, but no cigar," she said.

Not the first cigar Marisa had denied me for some male infraction.

Changing the subject, I said, "I need to talk to Scooter in person. Sometimes, under skillful face-to-face questioning, a suspect will break down and confess."

"How many times has that happened?"

"Never," I admitted. "But there's always a first time."

8.

The Left Coast

The next morning, I met with Tom Sullivan in his office. I told him about my current working theory of the case and said I wanted to go to Santa Monica to see Scooter Lowry.

"You going to straight out ask him if he killed his uncle?" Sullivan said.

"I hope to be a bit subtler than that," I answered. I was going to add, "That's why you pay me the big bucks." But I didn't want to remind him, in case things didn't work out, and he might not want to cut me a check.

"Okay, Jack," he said. "But fly coach, don't stay in a Ritz-Carlton, or order any menu item that says market price."

"I can live with that," I said.

Too bad though. I was looking forward to an expense-account surf-and-turf dinner at some fancy restaurant with a view of the Pacific.

I boarded a plane for the flight from Fort Myers to Los Angeles for a face-to-face session with Scooter. I brought Bill's manuscript to pass the time editing.

I didn't want to violate my agreement with Sullivan by flying first class, but I did opt for a main-cabin upgrade to a seat with extra leg room and priority boarding. The airlines had squeezed more seats into their coach cabins to the point where a man my size could barely fit. If that was a problem, Sullivan could take it out of my Christmas bonus.

I hadn't been to California in more than ten years, when I was after a murder suspect. I didn't find him, by all accounts he'd crossed into Mexico, but I did succeed in angering the Los Angeles Police Department by intruding upon their territory without permission. They found out I was there when I happened upon a three-car accident on the 405 Freeway and stopped to help. One of the motorcycle patrolmen on the scene took my report. For some reason, maybe to be collegial, I told him I was a detective from Chicago, and I was busted, resulting in a complaint to my supervisor, who said, "Serves you right for being a Good Samaritan, something I never do."

Once again, I decided not to tell local law enforcement I was coming. Explaining who I was and why I was there would be a hassle. If someone needed help, I'd call 911 anonymously.

The flight was full. I had an aisle seat. Looking out a window reminded me that we were up in the air, the province of birds, not people. A man next to me in the middle seat resembled the John Candy character Del Griffith in one of my favorite flicks, *Planes, Trains and Automobiles*. I didn't ask what he did for a living, but shower-curtain-ring salesman was a definite possibility. When he asked me, I told him I was an insurance salesman, a sure-fire conversation stopper. No one wants to be trapped into a comparison of whole-life versus term-life policies. That allowed me to get some editing done.

At LAX, I rented a black Dodge Charger GT muscle car with a 3.8-liter engine, a real beast, so I could hold my own on the freeways. It cost more than a Toyota Camry, but Sullivan seemed like a guy who understood the California car culture. If not, he could also deduct the upcharge from my bonus.

I drove to Santa Monica, daring anyone to get in my way, but no one did. The locals drove fast, but, for the most part, skillfully, probably because they'd been trained to navigate the congested roadways like Indy 500 racers, running wheel to wheel, hell-bent for leather. Chicagoans drove fast, too, but not as well, and Floridians mostly ran into one another, on the streets and in parking lots.

I checked into the Wyndham Santa Monica At The Pier at four o'clock local time, settled into my room, and thought about how best to approach Scooter Lowry. Given his background, it wasn't likely he'd flown to Naples, snuck into the Wilberforce house, and shot his uncle. But a hired gun could do that for him.

Google Maps told me Scooter lived in a house on Hart Avenue, a short walk from the beach. I drove over and found that the house was a tidy, tan-stucco bungalow with a red-tile roof. I pulled into the driveway, went to the front door, and rang the bell. If I'd brought a Bible, I could have told Scooter I was a Jehovah's Witness, asked him for permission to come in to talk about Jesus and then turned the conversation to homicide. Or I could have told him the truth about why I was there and observed his expression. Like the old gambler in the Kenny Rogers song, "I've made a life out of readin' people's faces."

But Scooter didn't answer his door. I decided to drive back to the Santa Monica Pier and have a look around. I didn't imagine I'd spot Scooter on the Ferris wheel, but if I cruised the bars, I might find him prepping for another DUI arrest. At minimum, I could locate something for dinner. It wasn't dinnertime in Florida, but I wasn't in Florida.

Strolling around the beach area, taking in the sights, I came upon a place called The Misfit Restaurant + Bar on Santa Monica Boulevard. Scooter's kind of watering hole, I figured. I walked inside, found an open barstool, and ordered a diet root beer and a sandwich.

The bartender was a young woman wearing a pink bikini top and skimpy white shorts. That wouldn't be a good look for my bartender, Sam, but I might suggest he wear a muscle shirt to increase his tips from the ladies. She had short blonde hair, a body that went well with her outfit, and a full-sleeve tattoo on her left arm, all colors and swirls, with a dragon's head spewing fire. Scary.

When she served my food, I asked, "Do you know Scooter Lowry?"

She scrunched her nose, as if she smelled an unpleasant odor, and said, "Are you a cop?"

"Not in California," I answered.

"Huh," she said. "Never heard of him."

True or not true, that was the question. They made portable lie-detector machines, but I didn't have one with me, so I tried another tactic: "Do you know that, under the California Penal Code, it's a felony to lie to a law enforcement officer?"

"I thought you said you weren't one here."

"That's in your favor," I said.

I went with a backup plan that always worked. I took a fifty-dollar bill from my wallet, put it on the bar, and said, "I'm known as a generous tipper when someone helps me out."

I turned in the direction of a commotion at the far end of the bar, two men wanting to hustle the same woman, apparently. When I looked back, the fifty-dollar bill had disappeared. If the bartending gig didn't work out, the young lady could put together a Vegas magic act, opening for Penn & Teller.

"Actually, now that I think about it, that name does sound somewhat familiar," she said.

I wanted to ask her where the fifty was hidden, but that would have been ungentlemanly.

I showed her a driver's license photo of Scooter on my cell phone. Tom Sullivan knew someone who knew someone at the California DMV who e-mailed the photo to me.

"Does he come in here?" I asked.

"Actually, he was here last night."

I produced another fifty, asked her for a pen, wrote my cell phone number on the bill and asked her to call me when he came in again.

"I can do that," she said.

This time, I watched to see where she put the bill. It went inside her bikini top. Neither Penn nor Teller had a hiding place like that. I finished my sandwich and went out into the balmy California night.

I was immediately knocked onto the sidewalk by a young woman on Rollerblades. She had brown hair done in braids and was wearing a white tee shirt and white shorts. The tee shirt said, "Don't Make Your Problem My Problem." An appropriate message for what had just happened.

She skidded to a stop, took out her earbuds, looked down at me, and said, "Oh geez, like, I'm soooo sorry, sir. Are you, like, hurt?"

When a young woman called you sir, she thought you were her father's, or maybe grandfather's, age. I stood up as agilely as I could and told her I was fine. If I needed to go to the ER, I'd wait until she was gone to preserve a shred of my virility. I didn't want her telling her friends, "Like, I totally plowed into this old dude and he, like, broke, like, lots of bones, and had to, like, be taken to the hospital where he, like, maybe was DOA, for all I, like, know."

Kids today. At least she could have, like, called the hospital to, like, check on my, like, condition.

I told her I was fine and she smiled and skated away. Discovering that I remained ambulatory, geezer that I was, I went into five more bars without finding Scooter, so I walked back to my hotel, called Marisa to say hi, and asked about Joe, because she was taking care of him in my absence. Joe always enjoyed staying with Marisa because she made gourmet cat meals for him such as poached salmon, diced roasted chicken, and, his favorite, hamburger gravy, which I also was partial to. It was always difficult to reacclimate Joe to my cooking, which mainly involved a can opener.

Then I killed some time by continuing my editing of the manuscript of *Stoney's Downfall*. I made only a few minor edits, nothing to do with grammar or punctuation because Bill was better with the native tongue than I was. Usually I just wrote some notations in the margins about police procedures or handgun calibers and the like. I suspected that Bill made those errors purposely, just to give me something to do.

After an hour, I put the manuscript aside, went to the hotel's exercise room, ran on the treadmill and lifted weights, trying, mostly unsuccessfully, to not stare at a young woman in yoga pants and a tank top climbing a StairMaster, and then ordered room service and watched one of my favorite sports movies, *Bull Durham*, on TV before drifting off to sleep.

The next morning, I asked the hotel desk clerk for a good place for breakfast.

"We've got a free buffet," the clerk, a skinny young man with a shaved head, earring, and runaway case of acne, told me. His name tag said Lester. "But if you want some decent food, and are willing to pay for it, I recommend Mazie's Café over on Pico."

Lester gave me directions and I walked to Mazie's. I could tell before going in that it was my kind of place. It was one of those classic diners that looked like an Airstream trailer, with shiny aluminum siding and colored neon tubing around the front door, like The Baby Doll's jukebox in Bill's novels and in real life. The name of the place was spelled out in flashing red neon in the window near the front door, along with the statement, "We Never Close." Hopper could have used Mazie's as a model for *Nighthawks*.

I walked in. There was only one open stool at the counter. All of the booths and tables were full. You walk into a restaurant at meal time and you're the only one there, beat feet out of the place.

I slid onto the stool. A middle-aged waitress with dishwater-blonde hair and the build of a WWF wrestler came over immediately, filled my coffee cup, and put a menu on the paper place mat in front of me. The menu had stains on it that looked like ketchup and gravy. Another good sign.

"Specials this morning, darlin', are biscuits with sausage gravy, rib-eye steak with eggs and hash browns, a western omelet, and a blueberry belgian waffle. Need a minute with the menu or are you ready to order?"

"Born ready, ma'am," I told her. "I'll take the biscuits with sausage gravy."

"You want fries with that or fruit?" she asked me.

I just smiled at her and she said, "Fries it is, sweet pea. And save room for the pecan pie à la mode."

I did as I was told.

After breakfast, I drove back to Scooter's house and rang the doorbell again. Same result as before, so I decided to head for the beach where I could show Scooter's picture to a girl or two or three sunning herself or playing volleyball. In the detecting biz, we call that canvassing a neighborhood. A less kind term would be voyeurism.

It was seventy-two degrees and sunny, with low humidity, according to the weather app on my cell phone. Ragged, wispy scud clouds scurried overhead. I was wearing a white polo shirt, jeans, running shoes, and Ray-Ban Aviator sunglasses. As I strolled along the beach, I noticed that everyone else was wearing Oakley sunglasses and bathing suits. Guess I didn't get the memo. Many of them had their sunglasses pushed up onto the top of their heads, a fashion statement that always seemed the height of foolishness to me. If you did that, you should be wearing a second pair to protect your eyes.

I didn't notice him come up behind me. Not Scooter Lowry, but a bodybuilder wearing a sleeveless tee shirt and cargo shorts, with his sunglasses on top of his bald head. I decided not to mention that. If I had biceps like his, I too would cut the sleeves off all of my tee shirts. Maybe my dress shirts too.

The man, who had a gold ring in his pierced left ear, studied me, tilting his head like a dog, in his case a pit bull, trying to make out what you're saying, and asked, "You the detective who's looking for Scooter Lowry?"

I said yes. I had no idea how he knew who I was. Maybe it was the Ray-Bans. Or the fact that I was several decades older than everyone else on the beach. Or maybe he knew that girl bartender at The Misfit. Or all of the above.

I guessed that he wasn't carrying a weapon because, given his outfit, I would have noticed the bulge in his shorts. Actually there was a bulge in his shorts, but not pistol-shaped. Guys like him didn't need to carry a weapon. He looked like he could bench press a Volkswagen.

"Scooter's a friend of mine," he said. "Why don't you tell me what this is regarding."

What this is regarding. He sounded like the receptionist at Alan Dumont's law firm in DC.

"I just want to follow up on a phone conversation we had," I said. "About his uncle."

He folded his massive arms over his chest and looked at me as if deciding whether to believe my story or to pick me up, flip me upside down, and pull apart my legs like a turkey's wishbone. Snap.

Then he slipped a cell phone out of the back pocket of his shorts, made a call, had a brief conversation I couldn't hear over the sound of the surf, and said, "You can meet with Scooter in twenty minutes at the Starbucks on Ocean Avenue."

Then he walked down the beach, his calf muscles bulging.

What a show-off.

9.

Huh?

Scooter was seated at an outside round metal table under a green umbrella at Starbucks, with a tall paper cup in one hand and a cell phone in the other, texting with his thumb, an excellent display of manual dexterity.

He looked just like his driver's license photo, and I knew from the DOB on the license that he was thirty-eight years old, but I would have otherwise guessed that he was a college frat boy, or a surfer in the middle of an endless summer. He had thin, long-ish blond hair and glowing bronze skin that said he'd never spent money on sunblock. Guess where his Oakley sunglasses were.

Marisa was a Starbucks aficionado. I was not. Whenever I went there with her, which was not often, I was confounded by the Starbucks argot. She always asked for, and I'm paraphrasing, "A grande-skinny-no-whip-pumpkin-spice-caramel" something-or-other, hold the something else. It was a secret society, like Scientology, and I was not an initiate. When it was my turn to order, I'd ask for a black coffee, and the young barista would stare at me as if I was hopelessly déclassé, or maybe the barista just didn't understand what I meant.

I walked over to Scooter's table and said, "Hello, Scooter. I'm Jack Starkey."

He ended his texting, looked at me, smiled, and said, "Join me. You wanna get coffee first?"

I took a seat and said, "No, these places scare me."

He didn't ask why.

"Have you ever seen a Kevin Costner movie called *The Body-guard*?" I asked him as he took a drink of his coffee.

"Yeah, with Whitney Houston. One of my all-time favorite flicks actually," he said.

"Which prompts me to ask about the Incredible Hulk you sent to find me."

"Stanley? He's not my bodyguard, he's a pal. I helped him buy a gym. In gratitude, he says he'll always have my back."

"I'm curious about how you knew I was in town and about how Stanley located me at the beach," I said.

"Word got around that a detective from Florida was asking about me in the bars," Scooter said. "Stanley was a skip tracer for a bail bondsman before I bought the gym. He can find people without much trouble. Are you comfortable at the Wyndham?"

I ignored that show-off comment and said, "When we spoke on the phone, I told you that your Uncle Henry had been shot in the head at his house in Naples."

"Right. Right. Right."

I've always thought that saying, "Right. Right. Right." should be at least a misdemeanor, along with wearing your sunglasses on your head. By that test, Scooter was a two-time offender. I continued, "But I didn't tell you the whole story."

"Uncle Henry is still dead, isn't he?"

Scooter's attempt at humor. He wasn't ready for stand-up at The Comedy Store.

"Very much so," I assured him. "The fact is, it looks like Henry was targeted, and not killed by a random burglar."

I'd taken the trouble to travel to Santa Monica to see Scooter's reaction to that news. He looked at me as if he couldn't process what I meant, and finally said, "Huh?"

During my long career as a homicide detective, I'd sat across from countless suspects in interview rooms, gauging their reaction to probing questions, such as, "Where were you on the night of the

twenty-seventh between the hours of eight P.M. and midnight?"
Or, "I know that you did it, I just don't know why, so fill me in."
Responses from guilty people ran from: "You're not implying that
I had anything to do with it, are you?" to "Unless you're arresting
me, I'm out of here," or "I want a lawyer." Scooter's "Huh?" most
likely meant I'd wasted a trip to California.

I took the red-eye back to Fort Myers that night, drove home,
slept for six hours, got up, showered and shaved, made coffee, then
met Marisa at her house to pick up Joe and tell her about my trip.

She met me at the front door with a hug and a kiss on the
lips, with Joe standing behind her. He walked over to me, rubbed
against my leg and meowed. I was glad to see him too. I should
have checked to see if the airport gift shop had a catnip mouse. I
picked him up, ruffled the fur on his head, and said, "Hey, big guy,
I missed you."

I realized I'd blown it with Marisa too. I should have stopped
by the Gucci store on Rodeo Drive in Beverly Hills. Next time, I'd
do better by both of them.

Marisa and I sat on her back patio with cups of espresso, which
I didn't mind drinking when she made it because I didn't have to
figure out how to order it. Joe was asleep on her lap, the turncoat.
I told her about my interaction with Scooter Lowry.

"Now you'll try to see the two nieces?" she asked.

"Starting with the one in Boston, Libby Leverton. Her husband, Stewart, is a real estate developer," as I said. "At first glance,
the Levertons don't seem to need inheritance money. But now that
Scooter is not the most likely suspect, that leaves the two nieces.
I'll go to Boston tomorrow, so Joe might as well stay here, if that's
okay."

Joe woke up, nuzzled Marisa's hand, and she began scratching
behind his ears, which made him purr as loudly as twin Evinrude
outboards. Clearly they'd do well together if I was taking a trip to
the moon. If I did, I'd better bring back some rocks.

10.

Can You Get Scrod Here?

But I wasn't going to the moon, I was going to Boston to see Stewart and Libby Leverton. I knew from my online research that they lived in a row house on Beacon Hill that was featured in an article about historic homes in *Boston Magazine*, and that, according to stories in the *Boston Globe*, they, like Henry, were active in the local charity scene. At first glance, it seemed unlikely they needed inheritance money. But a detective can't rely on first glances, so I was on a flight from Fort Myers airport to Logan airport.

It was cold in Boston when I arrived, thirty-one degrees with snow flurries. Having checked the weather in advance, I brought my leather bomber jacket. With the collar up, I thought I looked too cool for school. I'd been to Boston once before when I took my daughter, Jenny, to visit colleges during her senior year in high school. Ultimately she chose Stanford. Weather might have been a factor. She must have liked the Northern California climate because she also chose Stanford Law School. She now was an associate with the largest law firm in Chicago.

Jenny said that, while on a campus tour of Boston College, her student guide told her a Harvard joke: A businessman flew into Logan airport for the first time and, on the way to the city, asked the cab driver if he could get scrod in Boston, scrod being a generic term for a small cod, haddock, or any other local white fish. The driver, who was a moonlighting Harvard student, replied, "Yes, sir, you certainly can get scrod here, but I've never heard it referred to in the pluperfect tense before."

Jenny got the joke and explained it to me. It had been a long time since I studied the conjugation of verbs at Saint Francis High School, where the nuns rapped our knuckles with a wooden ruler for giving wrong answers, and sometimes just because they could.

My Boston cabbie was clearly not a Harvard student. He was a beefy guy with a ruddy face and bulbous nose, and he was wearing a Red Sox ball cap. He looked to be in his late fifties. Just for fun, I asked him if I could get scrod in the city. He said, "Yeah, sure. I recommend Legal Sea Foods." I guess he didn't know his colleague, that moonlighting Harvard student.

I checked into the Hyatt, went to my room, and called Libby Leverton. She answered on the third ring and I said, "Mrs. Leverton, this is Jack Starkey, the detective from Florida. We spoke on the phone earlier about the death of your uncle, Henry Wilberforce."

She hesitated, then said, "And I told you I know nothing about that. Is there some reason you're calling again?"

"I'm in Boston," I told her. "Better to talk about that in person."

As with Scooter, I wanted to check out her facial expression while I questioned her.

She agreed to meet me for lunch, suggesting, coincidentally, the Legal Sea Foods restaurant at Copley Place.

It was chilly and windy, but I walked to the restaurant from the hotel instead of taking a cab because I needed the exercise. I got directions from the desk clerk, who warned me that Boston streets were convoluted, gave me a map, marking the route with a red marker pen, and said it was lucky I wasn't going to try to drive there on my own because I might never arrive. That reminded me of the Kingston Trio song about Charlie, who got lost forever while riding the MTA.

The desk clerk's map was clear. I arrived at Legal Sea Foods on time, at noon sharp, went inside, and approached a woman seated alone in a booth. She was pretty and well put together, with short dark hair with streaks of grey. She was wearing a pink sweater, accented with a string of pearls and matching earrings, jewelry like that of Leila Purcell, chairwoman of the board of the Miriam Wilberforce Art Museum. I guessed that women of Libby's and Leila's social class wore pearls like California beach boys and girls wore Oakley sunglasses.

"Mrs. Leverton?" I asked.

"Yes, and you must be Detective Starkey," she answered.

I slid into the booth and said, "I'm investigating Henry Wilberforce's murder."

I watched her face closely. Her eyes widened, she gasped, put one hand on her chest, and said, "His murder? Oh, my god . . . you told me he was dead . . . I assumed it was because he was so old . . . how . . . where?" she asked.

"He was in his house in Naples, Florida," I told her. "During the night, an intruder broke in and shot him."

Libby teared up, took a handkerchief from her purse, and blotted her eyes, being careful not to smear her makeup. Either she didn't know about the murder or she acted in local playhouse productions.

"Do you know who did it?" she asked.

"Not yet," I told her. "Can you think of anyone who might want to kill your uncle?"

Without hesitating, she said, "Oh, Lord, no. Uncle Henry is . . . was . . . a very good man."

Out of left field, I asked, "How is your husband's business doing?" Thinking she might be caught unaware and let slip a motive for murder.

"What?" she replied. "Stewart's business? What can that have to do with my uncle's . . . murder?"

"I like to gather all the background I can," I said.

For example, did she or Stewart have a hit man in their contacts list.

The waitress arrived. Libby ordered a small salad. The restaurant did have a burger for me.

When the waitress departed, Libby said, "You were asking about my husband's business. Stewart is doing very well. His company is the biggest commercial developer in the Boston area."

"Interesting," I said, and it was, because it might mean that they didn't need Henry's money. Or it might not, given the ups and downs of the real estate development business. And it wouldn't be unusual for a man to keep a business problem from his wife so that she wouldn't think less of him. Whenever I failed to close a case, I didn't tell Claire.

Libby asked for details about my investigation, which I explained as we finished lunch, including the possibility of a professional assassin. She listened, shaking her head, tearing up again, and repeating her assertion that her uncle had no enemies. At one point in my narrative, she asked, "What do you mean, professional assassin?"

"A person who kills people for money," I explained.

She shook her head and said, "What a sad world we live in, Detective Starkey."

She seemed sincere. By the time we finished lunch, I was pretty much convinced that Libby was innocent. I didn't yet know about her husband, Stewart. Alan and June Dumont were better suspects at that point, if only because they'd been so elusive with me. I'd circle back to the Levertons later, if necessary.

11.

Honey Trap

I walked back to the Hyatt, my jacket keeping me warm enough, checked out, and caught a cab to Logan. This time, my driver was a young woman who told me she was a Boston College student.

"I went to Loyola in Chicago," I said. "Another fine Jesuit institution."

"I'm thinking of transferring to a nonsectarian school," she said, glancing at me in the rearview mirror. "Because of the church scandals, and all."

"I get that," I told her. "It's a troubling and complicated issue for people to deal with."

"Do you still go to church?" she asked me.

"Not in the sense that I show up at a building every Sunday. It's more of an internal kind of thing for me."

"Interesting," she said. "I'll have to think about that."

I'd booked a flight from Logan to Reagan national airport. My plan was to try to interview Alan and June Dumont and wing it from there. Sometimes, winging it worked. Other times, you were in for a hard landing.

I called Marisa and Sam from the airport while waiting for my flight. They assured me that everything was under control. I wished I could have said the same.

Just for fun, I had a reservation at The Watergate Hotel. Bob Woodward had a book out about the current president. His first book, *All the President's Men*, written with his fellow *Washington Post* reporter Carl Bernstein, told the story of President Richard Nixon's downfall which began with a break-in at the Democratic National Committee headquarters in the Watergate office complex.

My flight from Logan was delayed. When I arrived late at The Watergate, the desk clerk told me the hotel was overbooked and the only room available was the presidential suite, where I could stay at no additional cost.

"A Middle Eastern sultan I am not at liberty to name just checked out," he said.

"I hope you changed the sheets," I told him. "Hard to sleep with sand in the bed."

With a straight face, he assured me that the sheets, of course, had been changed.

I called Marisa using Facetime on my cell phone and walked her through my lodgings. There was a full kitchen, a butler's pantry, a dining room, a living room with a fireplace, a library, and four bedrooms. *All the President's Men* and Woodward's new book were not in the library. I checked the master bedroom. The sultan had not left behind any sand, or any of his wives.

"Plus, there is twenty-four-hour room service and a butler on call for all the suites, I was told."

"I don't know why you would ever leave," she said.

"I'll milk it as long as I can," I assured her. "Gotta hang up now and order a hamburger from room service."

"Tell them to do it with white truffle and béarnaise sauce. Or perhaps foie gras and hollandaise."

"I believe I'll go with American cheese," I said. "Velveeta, if they have it."

"Pearls before swine," she said.

I slept like a sultan, but without the harem, and then showered and ordered a stack of buttermilk pancakes with sausage links,

OJ, and coffee, which I ate at the long dining room table while wearing a thick white terrycloth robe with a hotel logo, which I was tempted to appropriate as a souvenir, plus another one for Marisa. But I didn't want to get put on the feds' no-fly list. The shiny mahogany table held two candelabras worthy of Liberace's piano top, fine china, crystal glassware, and silverware that was nearly heavy enough to require two hands.

A room-service kid delivered the food. My butler, who was waiting outside my door in the hallway, served it and stood at attention while I ate, which made me feel self-conscious, so I was careful not to burp.

"What did the sultan like for breakfast?" I asked him.

"I'm afraid that's confidential, sir," he answered.

"Did he have a food taster?"

He smiled. "One of the women, sir," he said.

"Better her than you."

"Not part of my service," he said.

I dressed in my grown-up outfit and took the hotel Mercedes to Alan's law firm, Chesney, Hartson, Dumont & Hamilton on Constitution Avenue. The driver was a man in his forties, it appeared, wearing a black chauffer's uniform.

"I suppose you drive a lot of famous people," I said. "Like a Middle East sultan."

"He flew over his own Rolls-Royce limo, along with three black Suburbans for his security people," he told me.

"Too bad," I said. "You missed a big tip."

"The sultan's people gave generous tips to the entire hotel staff, including me," he told me.

Even though I didn't have oil money behind me, I gave him a twenty when we arrived.

Alan Dumont's law firm was housed in a tall, glass-sided, high-rise building overlooking the National Mall. From the sidewalk in front of the building, I could see the Lincoln Memorial and the Washington Monument.

I found the name of the law firm on the lobby directory and took the elevator to the top floor, which opened into the firm's spacious reception area done up with expensive furniture, rugs, and paintings. It was hard to imagine that the partners could afford the overhead by doing honest work.

I approached the receptionist, a perfectly tailored young man, and said, "My name is Detective Jack Starkey. I'm here to see Alan Dumont."

"What is this regarding, if I may ask," he asked.

"You may," I answered. "Tell him the jig is up."

"Of course," the young man said.

He spoke into the phone, leaving out the jig-is-up part, I assumed. Then he instructed me to take a seat, asked for my beverage order, and said that Mr. Dumont's executive assistant would be with me momentarily. I declined a beverage because I'd adequately topped my tank at breakfast.

After about three days, or maybe it just seemed that long, a woman, turned out in a green linen skirt-suit with a cream-colored silk blouse, accented with pearls just like Libby Leverton and Leila Purcell, and black heels, appeared through a door in the back wall of the reception room and said, "Detective Starkey?"

She was in her forties, I'd estimate, and tall; stylishly cut black hair; smooth, tanned skin suggesting she'd recently returned from a sunny vacation or tanning salon; and tortoise-shell reading half-glasses hanging from a gold chain around her neck, all of this producing the look of a well-paid librarian who enjoyed a good time after work. If that was true, I'd definitely want a library card.

I stood to greet her and said, "Guilty as charged. Not unlike your boss."

She smiled. "Let he who is without sin cast the first stone."

Paraphrasing John 8:7, if I remembered my Bible verses correctly.

I liked her for that.

"Stone throwing aside, I'd like just a few moments of Mr. Dumont's time, if that can be arranged," I told her.

"Is this official police business?" she asked me.

"Let's call it unofficial," I told her.

She winked and said, "Official will get you an audience."

I winked back and said, "Official it is."

Now I liked her a lot.

She instructed me to follow her to a conference room. Along the way, she asked where I was staying in town.

"The Watergate," I answered.

She raised an eyebrow. "Is the crime scene tape still up?"

More points for her side. If she was carrying a gun, I might have asked her to dinner.

When we reached the conference room, she seated me at a table about twice as long as the dining room table in my hotel suite, nodded at a bar built into one of the walls, asked if she could fix a drink for me, which I declined, and left to speak with her boss about his unexpected visitor.

About five minutes later, a man appeared in the conference room doorway with a dour look on his face. He was tall, tanned (vacation with his assistant?), a bit overweight, jowly, and was wearing the de rigueur uniform of the Washington power elite: navy blue pinstriped suit, blue shirt with white collar, rep-striped tie, and black loafers with gold horse bits on them. His wardrobe said, "If you're not dressed like me, make it quick, I don't have time for the hoi polloi."

Without entering the conference room, Alan Dumont said, "I thought I made it clear when you called, Detective, that my wife knows nothing about your investigation. And neither do I. So I can't imagine why you are here."

"There's been a new development," I said.

"And that is?"

"Henry Wilberforce was killed by a professional assassin."

It was time to lay that on the conference table and see how he reacted.

"I can assure you that June is not a professional assassin," he said. "Nor am I."

If Alan Dumont was a contract killer, customers could probably not afford his hourly rate.

"I don't imagine that either of you are," I said. "But maybe your law firm has one on call for clients who are slow to pay."

He scowled. I hadn't seen anyone actually scowl in a while. He did it well. Maybe he practiced the look in the mirror.

"This conversation is over," he said. "You can direct any future inquiries to my personal attorney. You can get his card from the front desk on your way out."

With that, he turned and walked away, no doubt to get back to some white-collar felony he was aiding and abetting for a zillion dollars an hour.

Bingo! Alan Dumont, husband of June Dumont, who was one of Henry Wilberforce's three living relatives, an attorney himself, had just lawyered up.

I decided I'd try to speak with June by showing up on her doorstep. I flagged down a taxi and gave the driver the address of the Dumonts' house, which I got from Brandon Taylor. We got to the Dumont residence in fifteen minutes. The house was not much smaller than my hotel. I told the driver to wait, walked up steps to the front porch, and rang the bell.

A short, middle-aged Hispanic woman, with her grey hair in a bun, wearing a white maid's uniform, opened the door. She asked how she could help me, a variant of, "What is this regarding?"

"Please tell Mrs. Dumont that she has won the Publishers Clearing House Sweepstakes," I said.

The maid gave me an uncertain look. She didn't want to bother her mistress needlessly, but neither did she want to turn away a possible potful of cash, surely a cause for her termination.

She said, "Just a moment, sir," and closed the door.

I waited more than a moment. The cabbie used the time to stand outside the car and smoke a cigarette. Then the door opened and a woman who had to be June Dumont asked, with icy annoyance in her voice, "Now what's this about some sort of sweepstakes?"

It was cold, but June didn't invite me inside. I'd seen photos of her on the Internet taken from the society pages of newspapers and magazines. All of them were younger than she was now, an indication of the way powerful people can control their environments. The June of today remained attractive, with perfectly coiffed short blonde hair, smooth skin, blue eyes, a straight nose, and eyebrows created by a pencil, not Mother Nature. I wondered how much the body shop charged her for all that work. She was wearing a yellow sweater set and, of course, a strand of pearls with matching earrings.

"I think your maid misunderstood me, Mrs. Dumont. I'm Detective Jack Starkey from the Naples, Florida, Police Department. I assume that your husband told you that your uncle, Henry Wilberforce, has passed away."

"Yes, of course he did," she said. "We haven't been in touch for years, so I didn't know before Alan reported your conversation with him. Uncle Henry was very old, so I wasn't surprised. He had a long and happy life."

"The thing is," I said, noticing that I could see my breath, "he didn't die of natural causes."

"What do you mean?" she asked.

"I mean that he was murdered," I said. "In his winter home in Naples."

"How awful," she said.

There was a moment of silence, indicating that she did not want to know any details about her uncle's death, so I handed her my Naples PD business card and said, "If you feel you need any further information about that, you can reach me at this cell phone number."

"Okay," she said, and closed the door.

Maybe she was ordering the maid to prepare a pot of tea for us with those little crustless sandwiches you have to eat several dozen of to be satiated. After five minutes or so, as I stood there shivering, it became clear that I wasn't going to have high tea with June Dumont. And it was also clear, from the old gambler in me, that she knew more about her uncle's death than she was revealing.

A black sedan came up the street and pulled into the driveway. The car had some sort of markings on the doors that I couldn't make out. I assumed they ID'd the vehicle as belonging to some sort of private security service. The driver got out and joined me on the porch. He was wearing a blue blazer with a crest on the pocket that said Peterson Security Services. He was built like a fireplug, with a bald head and a ruddy complexion and spider-web veins on his nose, which most likely came from indulgence in alcoholic beverages. A bulge under his blazer indicated he was packing heat.

"I'm Dick Humphrey, with Peterson Security," he said, giving me the evil eye. "And you are?"

"Jack Starkey."

"So Mrs. Dumont said. A detective from Florida."

"She got it right."

"And you've registered your presence with the Metropolitan Police Department?"

"That's my next stop."

"Mrs. Dumont says she doesn't wish to speak with you any further, so it's time to move on," he told me.

He didn't say, "Move on or I'll put you in Boot Hill," but that was clearly implied.

"Tell me, Dick," I said, "where were you on the job before this gig?"

"Bethesda PD," he answered. "The pay and the hours are better now."

"I guess I'm done here," I said. "Wouldn't want to keep the lady of the house from doing whatever it is the idle rich do with their afternoons."

Now that Dick could tell I wasn't going to give him a problem, he relaxed and said, "Beats the hell out of me, pal. I work for a living."

I said, "Have a nice day," walked back to the taxi, and told the driver to return me to my hotel.

When I walked into The Watergate lobby, I noticed that my overnight bag was on the floor beside the front desk.

"What's this all about?" I asked the desk clerk, a man of about forty wearing the uniform of the hotel. He had the small, closely set black eyes and pointy nose of a weasel.

"I'm afraid we needed your room, Mr. Starkey," he said.

"But I have a reservation for one more day," I told him. "Any room will do. I don't require quite that much space."

"I'm sorry, but we are fully booked," he answered. "Perhaps the nearby Holiday Inn has a room. Would you like me to check?"

"Do they have a free breakfast?" I asked.

"I believe they do," he said.

"Never mind," I told him. "I'll find a Marriott, where I get rewards points, plus the free eats."

I considered ripping off his head and shitting down his neck, as my marine drill instructor liked to say. But that would have negatively affected my relationship with the Metropolitan Police Department, not to mention the hotel industry's lobbying organization, which could put me on their no-lodging list. It was clear that the hotel's Mercedes would not be available to take me to my next appointment, now that I was persona non grata, so I didn't bother to ask.

Alan Dumont was clearly a man of power and influence, and he was flexing his muscles by having me evicted from The Watergate. Making a point: Don't mess with me or suffer the consequences. His executive assistant, nice as she seemed, had ratted me out. She must have a good salary and benefits package. Dumont wasn't going to talk to me, and neither was June, so no reason to

hang around DC any longer, especially without a presidential suite
to keep me in the manner to which I'd become accustomed.

I decided to go home and think about what I'd learned on this
road trip, and what I had not. Sometimes that helped. Sometimes
it didn't.

I went into the hotel bar, done in mahogany and brass, with
framed, autographed photos of politicians and celebrities on the
walls, none of them Richard Nixon or his men, I sat on a stool, one
of five or six people in the place, called the airline and changed my
reservation to the next flight to Fort Myers, and killed time watching a hockey game on TV.

The game between the Washington Capitals and Detroit Red
Wings was not interesting enough to prevent me from noticing a
sexy young blonde wearing a skimpy black dress and spike heels
when she slid onto the barstool next to me, smiled, and asked if
I'd like some company. Maybe that description could be considered
sexist, but that was exactly what she looked like and, I guessed,
what she was going for. That sort of appearance didn't happen
accidentally.

A story that's told in Florida: An old man walks into a bar,
takes a stool next to a woman he doesn't know, and asks her, "Do
I come here often?"

I smiled back at the woman, didn't ask if she came there often,
and thought, *Maybe Alan Dumont is setting a honey trap for me
like the Russians did, using sex to gain the advantage on a male
target.* Headline in the *National Enquirer*: FLORIDA DETECTIVE
CAUGHT WITH HIS PANTS DOWN. The story accompanied by
a photo showing same.

"No thanks," I told her. "But say hi to Putin for me."

She gave me an enigmatic Mona Lisa smile, which might have
been significant, or it might not have.

While waiting for my flight, I remembered Marisa and Joe. I
found a gift shop in the terminal and bought Marisa a nifty snow

globe with a little White House inside. When you wound it up it played "Hail to the Chief." It was certain to occupy a place of honor on her living room fireplace mantel. Or maybe in her garage in a box of Christmas ornaments. Joe was harder to shop for. There were no cat toys, so I selected a children's book called *Pete the Cat* by Eric Litwin. The blue cat on the cover was wearing four white basketball shoes. There must be quite a story behind those shoes and about why the cat was blue. I couldn't wait to read the book to Joe to find out.

12.

The Dark Web

It was a 285-mile drive from Fort Myers Beach to Key West, the southernmost tip of the continental US. MapQuest said you could do that distance in five hours and fifteen minutes, but that didn't allow for someone driving a red '63 Corvette Stingray convertible with the top down and the kickass aftermarket Alpine stereo system providing traveling music. I made it in four hours and forty-five minutes. The Florida Highway Patrol must have been busy with more pressing matters.

The final leg of the journey was on the Overseas Highway, as US 1 was called as it island-hopped along causeways from Miami to Key West, where you ran out of continent. With the green, frothy Atlantic on one side and the calm blue Gulf of Mexico on the other, it was one of the most scenic roadways in the country. Along the way, I passed Islamorada, a village where Ted Williams, an avid sport fisherman, had a home. I got my first sailfish off Islamorada, trophy-size, the boat captain told me, but I released it; I didn't want it staring at me accusingly from a wall.

Reaching Key West, I drove to the Southernmost Point Buoy, a red, black, and yellow bullet-shaped concrete structure sitting on a square black marble pad at the corner of South and White-head Streets, and called Lucy Gates to confirm our appointment for lunch at Sloppy Joe's, the famous Duval Street bar where

Hemingway hung out. I had yet to find a bar in Key West where Hemingway did not hang out.

The Buoy was a font of information. Its lettering said, reading from top to bottom: "The Conch Republic," "90 Miles to Cuba," "Southernmost Point Continental USA," "Key West, FL," and "Home of the Sunset."

As I stood there thinking about how Marisa's father had made the perilous journey from Cuba to Miami during the Mariel boat-lift in 1980, a man asked if I would take a picture of him and his wife and two young children standing in front of the Buoy, which I did. The man thanked me and said they lived in Des Moines. He gazed out at the ocean and said, "You go any farther and you need a boat."

Presumably a more seaworthy craft than Marisa's father had floated in to Florida and freedom.

Lucy Gates was a young woman who helped me on my last Florida murder investigation. She was a world-class computer hacker who served three years in the Federal Correctional Institution in Tallahassee for transferring funds from someone else's bank account into her own in order to pay off her college loans. She intended to pay it back when she was able. The account owner was so wealthy that Lucy thought he wouldn't notice the unauthorized withdrawal, but his accounting firm did.

I got permission from a friend in the FBI to work with Lucy while she was still incarcerated to penetrate the dark web in search of someone killing people in Florida in a complex case involving offshore oil drilling in the Gulf of Mexico, corrupt state politicians, a Russian oligarch, and a father whose son was not getting enough playing time on his Little League team.

I needed Lucy's help again. Google for Dummies had taken me as far as it could. Lucy served her time and moved to Key West, where she operated a legit computer consulting business helping companies and government and private institutions with cybersecurity.

I found her at Sloppy Joe's seated in a booth with her laptop, probably working on a client project. Lucy was a pretty woman in her late twenties, with shoulder-length brown hair, an infectious smile, and wire-rimmed glasses. She was wearing a white tee shirt with the #MeToo logo symbolizing the anti-sexual-harassment movement, and jeans. We'd gotten to be friends during my last case, and I might have given her a greeting kiss on the cheek, but her tee shirt gave me pause. Probably needlessly, but a lot of men were on edge these days about their interactions with women, some justifiably so, some not. Movements are blunt instruments, not scalpels. So it goes.

I slid into her booth and said, "Last time I saw you, Lucy, you were wearing an orange jumpsuit. I like this outfit better."

She smiled and said, "Plus, the food's better on the outside. We gonna have some fun again, Jack?"

I'd given her an overview of my case when I called her, and now I began to fill in the details when a waitress arrived. Or it may have been a waiter. Key West was like that. I ordered one of the bar's famous Original Sloppy Joe sandwiches, with a side of onion rings and a diet root beer.

"I'll have what he's having," Lucy told the waitperson. "But make mine a diet Dr Pepper."

I finished the briefing and said, "So, for starters, I need to know everything you can find out about that niece and her husband in Washington, June and Alan Dumont. A power couple. At this point, they're at the top of my suspect list."

I told her everything I knew about the Dumonts. She thought about that and said, "Not a problem. Easier than hacking a presidential election. Which, as I might add, was a fine piece of work by the boys at the FSB."

The FSB was the unit of the Russian government responsible for cyber warfare.

When we finished lunch, I said, "So, Lucy, how goes your new life here?"

"Couldn't be better," she answered. "I've got more clients than I can handle, I love the outdoor life, and I'm in a relationship with a woman who captains a stone-crab fishing boat."

"Second chances," I said. "Eventually, if we're lucky, we get it right."

Lucy went home to begin her research and I drove back to Fort Myers Beach, beating my time on the way down by six minutes.

That night I went to The Drunken Parrot, wondering if we should have a Hemingway Look-Alike contest like Sloppy Joe's did each July to celebrate Papa's birthday and put up a brass plaque saying that Ernest drank at my bar whenever in town, even though I had no evidence that he ever was in Fort Myers Beach. I tried those ideas out on Sam. His response: "Let's not put lipstick on a pig."

I spent the next three days catching up on bar business and other chores and doing more book editing. I stopped by Tom Sullivan's office in Naples for an update and to hand in an expense report, which he signed without reading. I should have had the market-price lobster. I took Marisa to dinner at her favorite French restaurant and updated her on my investigation; she seemed more interested in her coq au vin.

The morning of the third day after my Key West trip, I was making a pot of coffee when my cell phone began playing the "Marines' Hymn." The caller ID told me it was Lucy Gates.

"That was fast," I said.

"Like shit through a Strasbourg goose," she replied.

Lucy was not your average female person.

"You find out anything useful?" I asked her.

"Only if you think learning that Alan Dumont seems to have a very big problem with the New England Mafia is useful."

"Wow. Tell me."

"Alan has a client, a shipbuilding company in Maine called Dirigo Steelworks. Dirigo being the state motto of Maine. It's Latin for 'I Lead,' referring to the time when Maine was the only state to hold elections in September. But I digress. Any-hoo, Dirigo was bidding on a navy contract to build a new class of destroyer. You can imagine what that contract would be worth. A lobbyist friend of Alan's told him that a man who lived in Providence, Rhode Island, could, for the right price, help grease the skids. How wasn't made clear. Don't ask, don't tell. Dirigo approved the payment, that kind of thing happens all the time in the defense contracting game, and the sum of six million dollars was wire transferred from one offshore bank account to another."

"Did Alan know the identity of the Providence skid-greaser?"

"Apparently not. The lobbyist, whose name is Sheldon Sharkey, believe it or not, was the middleman. Turned out that Dirigo didn't get the contract. And even though the fee was paid in full, the Providence guy said he was going to keep the money. Also turned out that the Providence guy, Tony 'Butterfingers' Russo, was a top lieutenant of one Larry 'Lucky Boy' Infante. Heard of him?"

I had. Infante was head of the New England Mafia. Coincidentally, another Larry Infante had been a minor league baseball player. Unless the Providence guy was originally from Venezuela, the two weren't related.

I loved Mob nicknames: Bobby "Buzzsaw" Marinara. Tommy "Icepick" Puttanesca. Louie "Joey Tire Iron" Langoustine. Sammy "Storm Drain" Alfredo. From their nicknames, you could imagine their weapons of choice, or where to look for a body. Jack "Hammer of Thor" Starkey would do quite nicely *pour moi*. I especially liked the name of *The Sopranos* character, Paulie Walnuts. You could envision him cracking walnuts with his bare hands to intimidate someone. You wouldn't want to send a guy called Alfonse "Bambi" Mostaccioli to collect your debts. *What's that you say, Bambi? Pay up or else? Yeah, right, kiss my ass and go back to yo' mama in the forest.* I knew a vice detective named Ed Lapidus. His nickname was Beano, which referred to his chronic flatulence. He was a good cop, but you didn't want to ride with him.

"Infante is the godfather of the New England Mob," I told Lucy.

"Right. Well, as you can imagine, Dirigo was pissed about not getting the destroyer contract and they wanted their six mil back."

"Uh oh."

"Right. Rule Number One is never ask the Mob for a refund. That lobbyist I mentioned, Sheldon Sharkey, is among the missing, as is a guy named Daniel Danko, vice president of government relations for Dirigo. Both are probably taking a dirt nap with Jimmy Hoffa."

"Wowzer. How'd you find all that out?" I asked her.

"Like the CIA, I never reveal sources and methods," she told me. "Let's just say that if I wanted to read all of your texts and e-mails, hack into your bank records, get all your Marine Corps fitness reports, and know what restaurants you've dined at recently using your credit card, I could."

"Scary."

"By the way, did you really get busted from captain to lieutenant in the marines for trashing a bar in Subic Bay?" she asked me.

"I didn't like being a captain anyway," I said. "Too much responsibility. So where does that leave Alan Dumont?"

"Infante wants him to find another one of his clients willing to hire his Mob family as a fixer for a big fee," Lucy said. "And more after that, most likely."

"Assuming that's true, I wonder how it could relate to the murder of Henry Wilberforce," I said. "Why would Dumont and his wife need Uncle Henry's money?"

"Now that's a conundrum," Lucy said. "As a partner in his law firm, he makes north of three million a year in salary, plus big bonuses. And the Dumonts have a twenty-million-dollar investment account being managed by one of the big investment banks in New York. The portfolio is doing very well. It's my opinion that, even if Alan would want to help June get a nice inheritance from her uncle, they don't need the money enough to have Henry killed, and Alan has his hands full dealing with the Mafia thing."

"That's a lot to think about, Lucy," I said. "Send me your bill and I'll see it's paid promptly."

I had to agree with her conclusion, which meant that Stewart and Libby Leverton, the Boston socialites, were now at the top of my suspect list.

13.

My Usual Life

I hadn't been paying much attention to my bar. Bill Stevens was reminding me that the deadline for finishing my editing of *Stoney's Downfall* was approaching. I was certain that Marisa was feeling neglected. Joe too. And I was tired of going from city to city, living out of a suitcase, without much to show for it, investigative-wise.

I'd been eating very well while traveling on my Naples PD expense account and exercising only sporadically. Life on the road was like that.

After breakfast aboard *Phoenix*, I drove to a nearby beach and did a three-mile run. A pair of dolphins frolicked alongside my route. Then I dropped to the sand and did fifty push-ups and sit-ups. Passersby could see that I was still in my Marine Corps fighting form—for all they knew.

I drove back to my boat, changed into jeans and my Cubs tee shirt, and went to The Drunken Parrot. It was midmorning. A few regulars who always knew it was five o'clock somewhere were getting an early start on their buzz, which would build through the afternoon and into the evening, until they resided in a world where they were kings, adored by their subjects, and their kingdoms dominated the known world. Dean Martin said he felt sorry for people who didn't drink because, when they woke up in the morning, that was as good as they were going to feel all day. Before rehab, I thought that too.

I found a ladder in the storeroom, carried it outside, and climbed up to check out the new roof. It looked like a roof. The first heavy rain would tell me if the money it cost was well spent.

Then I went into the office and paid bills. Sam was behind the bar polishing glasses, and Alice was in the kitchen, getting ready for the lunch crowd. When I'd worked my way through the bills, I drove to Café Provence to meet Marisa for lunch. She liked French food more than I did, but I discovered that a croque monsieur was a grilled ham and cheese sandwich, so I was covered.

I found her seated at an outside table on a deck overlooking Estero Bay. I took a seat at her table and asked, "Are you alone, sweet cheeks, or is your boyfriend coming?"

"You better leave because, even though he's not the man he used to be, he carries a gun," she replied.

"As it happens, so do I, so I'll take my chances."

She smiled. "Maybe his gun is bigger than yours."

A waiter wearing a long white apron came outside to take our orders. He spoke with a heavy French accent. I suspected he was from New Jersey and was faking it.

"So, about your case," Marisa said. "Did the butler do it in the library with the candlestick?"

"Would that it were so."

"Any suspects other than the butler?" she asked.

I gave her an update and told her that, through the process of elimination, Stewart and Libby Leverton in Boston were now my prime persons of interest.

"It would be nice to see a woman of Libby's high social status brought low," Marisa commented. "I'm just sayin'."

"I go where the evidence leads me," I replied.

"Wherever it leads, it's amusing to imagine how she would fare among the general population of a state penitentiary."

"I hear you. But she's not there yet."

Our food arrived. We spent the rest of the time chatting about Marisa's real estate business, about the sad state of national politics, which had always been a downer, but currently seemed to have hit a new low in the history of the republic, and about the upcoming Major League Baseball season. Actually we didn't talk about baseball, I did, and I'm not certain Marisa was fully paying attention, unless she was taking notes on her cell phone, and not texting someone about another subject.

Back at my bar, I took a mug of coffee to my usual booth and went back to editing *Stoney's Downfall*.

Twenty minutes later, I looked up from the manuscript to see a man I didn't know standing beside my booth. He was late middle-aged, pink-faced, shaped like an eggplant, with a thin comb-over, and was wearing a tan shirt with a black embroidered name tag that told the world, or the small portion of it that paid attention to him, that his name was Harvey. Dennis Miller said if you wore a name tag to work, you'd made "a serious vocational error." When I was a patrolman, I wore a nameplate, proving that Dennis Miller was right. Being a plainclothes detective was better.

Harvey was holding a clipboard. "Mr. Starkey?" he asked.

"Guilty as charged. What's up, Harv?"

"I'm with the Fort Myers Beach Public Health Department," he said, in the high-pitched voice of a castrato. "I'm here for a periodic inspection of the premises."

He meant surprise inspection, which is how they also did it in the marines.

"I wish you'd have let me know you were coming," I told him. "We'd have mopped up the raw sewage from the kitchen floor and disposed of the rat carcasses."

Harvey didn't react to my little joke. He looked at his clipboard and said, "When we were here three months ago, the grease trap in the kitchen needed cleaning, the walk-in cooler was four degrees too warm, and a dead cockroach was found in the storeroom."

I wasn't willing to give up on my comedy routine and told him: "The last person who said that didn't leave here alive, Harvey, my man."

"Excuse me?" he said, looking alarmed.

"Feel free to look around, at your own risk," I said.

I was confident that Sam had taken care of those items, if they were even real, and that Harvey would find new infractions. Singers had to sing, dancers had to dance, street cops had to give out tickets, and city inspectors had to find violations, or they might have to work for a living.

14.

Be Careful Out There

"**M**aybe you should give it a rest for a while, Jack," Tom Sullivan said after I updated him on my investigation as we sat in his office in Naples police headquarters. I couldn't blame him. My performance so far had not been Hall of Fame quality.

"What's with the full-dress uniform?" I asked him.

"Funeral of a retired sergeant who died of a heart attack," he told me. "Twelve years ago, he got the department's Medal of Valor for running into a burning house to save an entire family. So it's a funeral with full honors."

Just like my brother, Joe, but the sergeant survived.

Sullivan spread his hands and said, "I'm serious about you taking a step back from the case, Jack. If you get killed while on my payroll, there'll be a lot of paperwork, and I really hate paperwork."

But it was too soon to quit. A good rule is, it's always too soon to quit. When I was a boy, discouraged about something or other, my father read a quotation to me by Teddy Roosevelt. Teddy said that it was better to try and fail than to be one of "those cold and timid souls who neither know victory nor defeat." This wouldn't be the first time I'd tested that maxim.

"If you don't mind, I'd just as soon keep after it," I said. "I don't plan on dying."

"Who does?" he asked.

"Not Henry Wilberforce."

He stroked his chin for a moment and said, "True enough."

"I need to have another run at the Levertons in Boston," I told him, having explained why Scooter Lowry and June Dumont now seemed less likely suspects.

He leaned back in his chair, laced his fingers behind his head, was silent for a moment, and then said, "Okay, Jack, stay on the case. But be careful out there."

I recognized that as a reference to one of my favorite cop TV shows, *Hill Street Blues*. Actor Michael Conrad, playing Sergeant Phil Esterhaus, always said, "Let's be careful out there," at the end of every roll call. When I was a rookie patrolman, our sergeant always said, "Now get the fuck out of my face and don't get your dicks caught in a wringer."

Equally effective. We had some female officers, but they knew what he meant.

THREE MONTHS EARLIER

15.

Co-conspirators

Nelson Lowry, Libby Leverton, and June Dumont, who were, as far as they knew at that time, the only living heirs to the vast Wilberforce family fortune of Chicago, were seated around a long mahogany table, so highly polished that their visages were reflected on its gleaming surface, in the conference room of the Washington, DC, law firm of Chesney, Hartson, Dumont & Hamilton on Constitution Avenue. Alan Dumont was the group's host, and Libby Leverton's husband, Stewart, was in attendance as well.

Yellow legal pads and gold Cross pens were placed on the table before each of them. Bottles of chilled San Pellegrino water rested on sterling silver-and-cork coasters.

"Does anyone recall when they last saw Uncle Henry?" June asked. "Was it before or after Miriam died?"

"I saw him at Aunt Miriam's funeral in Lake Forest, maybe ten years ago," Libby said. "You and Scooter weren't there."

"I had some sort of conflict," June said.

"Me too," Scooter said.

"You probably had a hangover, Scooter," June said. "So, for me, it was at your daughter's wedding on Martha's Vineyard, Libby, whenever that was."

"Twelve years ago," Libby told her.

"I had a conflict for that too," Scooter said. "Frankly, I can't remember the last time I saw our uncle."

Libby was turned out that afternoon in an ice blue Vera Wang dress and black Jimmy Choo peep-toe heels. June had chosen a charcoal wool three-button Valentino pants suit, a rose-gold Cartier Love necklace with matching earrings, and red eel-skin Dolce & Gabbana sling-back pumps. Scooter, looking like a yacht club commodore, wore a double-breasted, brass-buttoned navy-blue blazer, pleated white linen slacks, a pink oxford-cloth shirt with button-down collar, open at the neck, and Top-Siders, worn sockless, as was de rigueur for that sort of outfit.

Alan rose from his chair at the end of the table and stood gazing through the conference room's wall of windows at the National Mall. This vista always pleased him.

The family was gathered in the conference room because Libby had attended Vassar with a woman named Trish Conroy, who was married to the CEO of United Airlines, which was headquartered in Chicago. Libby and Trish had remained close friends after graduation. One week earlier, Trish had e-mailed a link to a *Chicago Tribune* article about Henry Wilberforce to Libby, with a message: "Libby, I thought you should know what your Uncle Henry is up to these days." The article described a number of extremely generous gifts of money and personal property Henry had been bestowing upon people and institutions in recent months, in addition to the planned giving of the Henry and Miriam Wilberforce Foundation.

Libby showed the e-mail to Stewart and then, on his advice, forwarded it to Scooter and June, and now, here they all sat, their sole agenda being to figure out what if anything might be done to stop their uncle from squandering any more of his fortune, which, they assumed, would be *their* fortune when Henry passed away.

Alan turned from the window at the sound of a secretary entering the conference room. She was pushing a cart bearing coffee, tea, soft drinks, orange juice, bottles of chilled San Pellegrino, croissants, bagels, a plate of lox with cream cheese and chopped red onions and capers, and fruit. The ceramic coffee mugs bore the name of the firm; the teacups and saucers were made of bone china with a royal Ming tree pattern.

"Please, help yourselves," Alan said as he shot a cuff to check his Patek Philippe. It was three fifteen, fifteen minutes past the designated starting time of this meeting. "We'll wait a few more minutes for Ray Gillis to arrive, then we'll begin with or without him," Alan told them.

"For a retainer of ten K a month, plus expenses, this Gillis person shouldn't keep us waiting," Scooter said testily.

"I second that," Libby added, clicking her long red nails on the tabletop to display her annoyance.

"What've you got for us, Alan?" Scooter asked. He'd been doodling smiley faces and rows of second-grade-penmanship circles on his note pad. "Any ideas, or are we just here for a familial circle jerk?"

"As you'll see, Alan has a very good idea," June said.

June had been raised on Philadelphia's Main Line, where the term "circle jerk" had never come up during social gatherings. She wasn't entirely certain what it meant, but coming from Scooter Lowry, she was reasonably certain she didn't want to know.

Alan checked his watch again, tapped a manila file folder lying before him on the table, and said, "Mr. Gillis has given me a comprehensive report. I'll summarize it for you while we're waiting, and then . . ."

The same secretary who'd brought in the snack cart opened the conference room door and announced, "Mr. Gillis is here, Mr. Dumont. I have him in the reception area."

"Show him in, Cindy," Alan told her. Then to the group: "I think you'll agree our man has earned his fee."

Cindy reappeared a moment later with Ray Gillis in tow. Libby leaned toward Scooter and said, "Our man seems to be mainly interested in investigating young Cindy's ass."

"Can't blame him for that," Scooter said as he watched Cindy turn and exit the conference room.

Ray Gillis was indeed observing the ebb and flow of Cindy's buttocks moving beneath the tight fabric of her pink linen skirt, which made him momentarily forget where he was, and why.

Alan rose to greet Gillis with a handshake, then gestured him toward the opposite end of the conference table where a laptop computer was connected to a projection device aimed toward the far wall. Alan picked up a remote control from the credenza, pushed a button, and a white screen descended from the ceiling.

"This is Mr. Raymond Gillis," Alan said as Gillis settled in before the computer, withdrawing a flash drive designed to look like a Swiss Army knife from his jacket pocket. "He has undertaken a number of assignments for our firm in the past. We've always been pleased with the results."

"Good to meetcha, you all," Gillis said as he inserted the flash drive into a USB port on the side of the computer. The cousins did not return the greeting; they would wait to see how pleased they were to meet *him*.

"I'll use visual aids in my presentation," Gillis said as he moved the mouse on the tabletop and double-clicked it. As he did, a large color photograph appeared on the screen. It showed Henry Wilberforce, wearing yellow pajamas, a white terrycloth robe, and a Panama hat, watching workmen operating heavy equipment at a beach. A bulldozer was moving a pile of sand, and a crane was lowering a boulder onto a retaining wall jutting out into the water. The foreground of the photo was out of focus, as if the photographer was using a long lens.

"I took this April 9th at the Lake Forest town beach," Gillis told them.

"So Henry's watching some guys working at the beach," Libby interjected. "That's important *because*?"

"You're seeing a beach improvement project," Gillis explained. "Price tag, ten million six for reinforcing the seawall, resanding the beach, building a new pavilion, expanding the parking lot, and purchasing a fleet of eight-foot sailing dinghies for a children's instructional program. Funding for the project had been cut from the city budget for the past three years. Then Mr. Wilberforce became involved."

Scooter, a sailor, was impressed with Gillis's attention to detail: eight-foot dinghies, not just little sailboats. "He's fucking killing us," he sighed, slumping back in his chair.

"This is more serious than I thought," Libby whined.

"Copy that," Stewart added. "Something *must* be done. And *soon.*"

Gillis moved the mouse, and another photo appeared: Henry standing in an art gallery with a well-tailored woman in her seventies. They were looking at a large, framed oil painting showing a bed of purple flowers. Henry this time wore the uniform of a Pullman train conductor. His hand was on the woman's shoulder.

"Maybe Uncle Henry's getting some nooky," Scooter joked, adding, "I'd say that babe's sell-by date expired some time during the Eisenhower Administration."

"Mr. Wilberforce is with Elizabeth Broomfield in a gallery at the Lake Forest Art Museum," Gillis told them. "She is the widow of Elias Broomfield, who founded the Broomfield Iron and Steel Company of Gary, Indiana. She's chairwoman of the museum's acquisition committee."

Libby said, "I'm not liking the word 'acquisition' in her title."

"The painting is by Vincent van Gogh," Gillis said. "It recently sold at auction at Christie's in New York for $42.5 million to an anonymous buyer, presumably your Uncle Henry, who then donated it to the Lake Forest museum. It was their biggest gift ever."

"Jesus H. Christ!" Scooter shouted. "He buys a painting like that for a small-town museum? What'd they have before, a few Audubon prints and some watercolors by locals who always wanted to paint? Now he'll have to buy them an alarm system too! Maybe hire a guard!" He leaned forward, elbows on the table, burying his face in his hands. "It's just not right, giving all that money to . . . to people who aren't even family."

Libby stood, went to the cart, picked up a croissant, and took a bite. Then, remembering her no-calorie diet, which basically required her to live on air like an orchid, she turned her back to the conference table and spit the bite into a cloth napkin. She took a Diet Coke and huffed, "Well, if Uncle Henry runs out of money, *I'm* not taking him in."

Next came a series of photos showing Henry entering a restaurant, getting into the back seat of a chauffeured limousine, reclining on a lounge chair on his back patio while reading a book, and flying a kite in a park with a man dressed in butler's mufti standing beside him. In the photos, Henry was dressed as an equestrian with jodhpurs and riding boots, a World War I-era aviator with leather helmet and goggles, a cowboy with chaps and ten-gallon hat, and Santa Claus.

"As distressing as all this . . . *generosity* . . . is, and as loony as he looks, is there anything actually actionable here?" Libby asked. "I mean, the man can give his money to anyone he wants, can't he? And dress up however he likes?"

"Maybe we should just have him whacked," Scooter said, looking at Gillis.

"Try to be *somewhat* relevant," Libby said. "This isn't an episode of *The Sopranos.*"

"Continue, please," Alan told Gillis.

"People say that Henry often doesn't know what decade it is," Gillis said. "And that he talks to an imaginary dog named Buddy."

"I remember that he told me once that he had a golden retriever named Buddy when he was younger," Libby said. "He showed me pictures. That dog must have died by now."

"If I may continue," Gillis said.

"Go on," Alan told him.

Next in the slide show was a photo of Henry riding in the back seat of a Lake Forest police cruiser. He was smiling broadly.

"He got arrested?" June asked hopefully.

"No," Gillis answered. "He takes walks and sometimes gets lost. The local police department watches out for him and takes him home. I know this because a sergeant on the force used to be a Chicago cop when I was."

Alan held up the file folder. "We have copies of Henry's tax returns for the past seven years, his credit card and bank statements, and telephone bills."

Scooter indicated Gillis, still seated at the end of the conference table, with a nod of his head, and said, "Man, I hope you never sic this guy on *me*."

"How do you know we haven't?" June asked.

Scooter looked at her.

"Kidding," June added, after a pause just long enough to make her cousin wonder.

"What we don't have yet are Henry's medical records," Gillis told them. "I'm working on that. So I can't tell you at this point what has caused this behavior. Maybe the onset of Alzheimer's, or a brain tumor, or a stroke . . . Or maybe he just read his Bible, you know, the part about Jesus saying it's easier for a camel to go through the eye of a needle than for a rich man to get into heaven."

Scooter held out his palms in a pastoral gesture. "Let us pray that disease and not the New Testament is responsible for Uncle Henry's attempt to lead us all into the Land of Abject Poverty. Not that any of us needs the money, of course. But I hate to see it being pissed away, and you know what they say about never being too rich."

"Amen to that," Libby said. Stewart nodded his agreement.

Scooter looked at the others and wondered: *Or does one of you actually need our uncle's dough?*

His report complete, Gillis ejected the flash drive, and stood. As he did, his suit coat flapped open, revealing a shoulder holster holding a big black pistol.

"Excellent job, as always," Alan told Gillis. "Now, if you will excuse us . . ."

When Gillis was gone, Scooter asked Alan, "What're the next steps, counselor?"

"Securities law is my area of expertise," Alan answered. "I've consulted with one of my partners who does estate planning, wills, and trusts and such, as well as other kinds of family matters relevant to our situation. Giving him a hypothetical fact situation, of course."

"Involving a hypothetical old fart who is hypothetically butt-fucking his hypothetical heirs," Scooter said, looking as distressed as he was.

Ignoring this, Alan continued: "He explained that there is well-established precedent for a family member to petition a probate court for a mental competency hearing. Your petition must meet a threshold of behavior calling into question the person's ability to function on his own. If the petition is approved, a judge or jury reviews the evidence, hears testimony, and decides whether or not the court should appoint a legal guardian. Often the guardian is a family member."

He paused, then added, "It wouldn't be easy. There is a fine line between incompetent and eccentric. We need more than colorful costumes and largesse. There must be evidence of a substantial loss of mental faculties, whatever the cause, to the extent that Henry is clearly unable to take care of himself. And possibly that others are taking advantage of him."

"People like us, you mean," Libby said.

Alan shot her a disapproving look and said, "An additional complication is that Henry has a household staff that looks after him. We'd have to show that, even with this assistance, he's not able to function on his own."

"And how exactly do we obtain that sort of evidence?" Stewart asked.

Alan walked to the credenza and poured a cup of coffee. "Ray Gillis is very skilled at that sort of thing," he told them. "He assures me that he can go deeper with his investigation, using covert means we don't need to know about, if we tell him to."

"So moved," June said.

"Seconded," Stewart said.

The vote was unanimous.

"So what's the timing for all this?" June asked.

"Raymond estimates that his investigation will take two or three months to do it right, possibly longer," Alan answered. "After that, one or all of you would file the probate court petition. My partner said that, depending upon the court's backlog, it could take anywhere from six months to a year to get a decision."

"By which time Uncle Henry will have used our money to solve world hunger, as well as the problem of clean drinking water on the African continent, and to put out the wildfires in the Amazon rain forest," Scooter said. "Bill and Melinda Gates will be happy for the help."

"Perhaps we need a timelier solution," Stewart said, and everyone looked at him. He paused and added, "I'll have to think about what that might be."

"I suggest that we direct Raymond to begin his research, and go from there," Alan told the group.

Everyone agreed, and the meeting was adjourned.

They all stood to leave. Scooter picked up the unused Cross pen in front of him and put it into his jacket pocket. Then he picked up Libby's, who'd been sitting beside him, and put that one in his pocket too.

"Did you notice that Mr. Gillis was packing heat?" Scooter asked Libby and Stewart as they rode the elevator down to the lobby.

Stewart had noticed.

"Maybe Alan has a backup plan in mind, in case the probate court thing doesn't work out," Scooter commented as the elevator doors opened on the ground floor. "Wouldn't it be a shame if Uncle Henry had an accident."

"Whatever works," Stewart said as he and Libby stepped out of the elevator ahead of Scooter, her heels clicking on the marble floor of the lobby.

Walking behind her, Scooter reflected that his cousin Libby still had a very nice body, thanks, he imagined, to her personal trainer, plastic surgeon, and a diet consisting largely of kale, tofu, and coconut water. Even though she was more than a decade older than he was, and family, he'd still very much enjoy playing hide-the-salami with her, given the opportunity. Scooter was nothing if not an equal-opportunity lover.

THE PRESENT TIME

16.

An Unexpected Visitor

Marisa and I were seated in my usual booth at The Drunken Parrot, having coffee and chit-chatting, when she looked up and asked, "Who's that classy chick in the Chanel knit cardigan set, Jimmy Choo Mirren 85 soft patent leather ankle boots, wearing a string of pearls with matching earrings, Mikimoto is my guess, and carrying a Hermes Himalayan crocodile Birkin bag?"

When it came to ladies' fashion, Marisa knew her stuff. I looked toward the bar and saw, to my great surprise, Sam talking to a woman it took me a moment to recognize. If a woman dressed like she was had ever come into The Drunken Parrot before, I wasn't there to see it.

It was none other than Libby Leverton, one of Henry Wilberforce's two nieces, come all the way from Boston.

Sam nodded toward me and Libby walked over to our booth. I stood and said, "You've come a long way for our happy hour, Libby."

She smiled. "I hear it's a very good one."

"Libby, this is my friend Marisa Lopez," I said. "Marisa, this is one of Henry Wilberforce's nieces."

I moved to Marisa's side of the booth and said, "Please join us."

Libby slid in where I had been sitting and said, "Pardon me for just dropping in like this, Detective Starkey. But I have something I need to discuss with you and I thought it better to do it in person."

Marisa looked at her wristwatch and said, "You'll have to excuse me, I have a house showing."

I stood so she could get out of the booth. When she was gone, I sat down and Libby looked at me, hesitated, then said, "I shouldn't be telling you this."

Which was a guaranteed way to get my full attention. I made a mental note to tell Bill Stevens that that would be a great first line for a novel. How could you not keep reading?

"I'm afraid I wasn't entirely straightforward with you when we met before," Libby continued.

"In what way?" I asked.

"I really didn't know that Uncle Henry was dead before you told me," she said. "But, several months before your visit to Boston, I was called to a family meeting at Alan Dumont's law firm in Washington. Alan is the husband of my cousin June. Alan, June, and Scooter Lowry, who is my other cousin, were there, in a conference room, along with a private detective Alan had hired, a most disagreeable man, to follow Henry around and document what we heard was his odd behavior. I was opposed to that, but I was outvoted. June had found out, I don't know how exactly, that Henry was giving away large amounts of money. She said that, as his only heirs, we should do something about it. The detective had a list of some of Henry's recent gifts, and photos of him around Lake Forest, wearing outlandish costumes. Alan said we could petition the Lake County Probate Court in Illinois to have Henry declared mentally incompetent to handle his own affairs, and have June appointed as his guardian."

"And you did that?" I asked her.

"No," she said. "Alan told us that the proceeding could take a very long time. Scooter was very upset about that. He's never made much of himself, truth be told. It was clear that he really needed our uncle's money. When the meeting ended, Scooter said, 'Wouldn't it be a shame if Uncle Henry had an accident.' He didn't mean it would be a shame, I'm certain. Then Uncle Henry died, even before that detective finished his work looking for proof

Henry couldn't take care of himself, so there was no reason for the court petition."

She paused, looked down at her hands, then up at me, and said, "Well, I never imagined that Scooter was capable of harming anybody, but . . ."

"But now you think he might have?"

"I don't know. I really don't. I hate to even *think* it's possible that Scooter could kill Uncle Henry, or have him killed."

"What about your cousin June?"

"To me, June is less likely than Scooter to commit such a horrible crime. She and Alan are very well-off financially."

"Thank you for telling me this, Libby," I said. "I'm glad you did, despite your reservations. I'll look into Scooter's possible involvement in your uncle's death."

I didn't say I would look at Scooter *again*.

"Please let me know what you find," she said. "One way or another, it will put my mind at rest."

"Can I give you a ride to the airport?" I asked her.

"Stewart arranged for me to use his company's airplane, and he hired a car and driver for me here," she said.

We stood and she left to fly back to Boston without having to go through the TSA line.

It was interesting that neither she nor Scooter nor Alan Dumont had suggested that someone other than one of the would-be heirs was responsible for Henry's murder. Which told me I was on the right track.

"So it's back to California to see Scooter Lowry," Tom Sullivan said when we met in his office later that afternoon.

"I have no idea if Libby Leverton is telling the truth about Scooter," I said. "But I need to check it out before drilling down on the Levertons."

Drilling down. Showing off my high-tech knowledge.

At that point, I felt like the Duncan Yo-Yo I had as a boy, being jerked up and down my suspect list.

"What will be your approach this time, given that the first go-round apparently didn't work?"

"When I figure that out, you'll be the second to know," I told him.

"And who will be the first?"

"Me."

I knew that Cubby Cullen would be interested in the new developments, so I called him. As I began to tell him about them, he cut me off and said, "You know, Jack, I can focus better when there's food in the vicinity."

I couldn't argue with that concept. We met at a little place called Pastrami Dan's in Naples. As we stood in line at the counter, Cubby said, "I just had my annual physical. Gotta watch my cholesterol level, so I'm just having one sandwich."

That was his problem. I got my usual two.

As we tucked into our sandwiches, I updated Cubby on my investigation, with all of its complications. He listened with interest, pausing to wipe the pastrami juice from his chin with the back of his hand, and asked, "Do you think this Scooter fellow has the skills to pull off a pro-style hit like that?"

"Nothing in his background indicates that he does," I answered. "But he has a friend who might. A big guy who has Scooter's back. He doesn't seem like a killer, either, but it's possible. I need to find out."

"Did your computer hacker lady turn up anything incriminating about Scooter?"

"She didn't. But if this pal, or Scooter himself, is responsible for Henry's murder, there wouldn't necessarily be any message traffic about the crime."

"In a situation like that, you need a confession," Cubby said. "Short of waterboarding, how you gonna pull that off?"

"The reason I offered to buy you that cholesterol torpedo, Cubby, is that I was hoping you'd tell me."

Cubby finished his sandwich, blotted his chin with a napkin this time, used the napkin to wipe a gob of mustard from his uniform shirt, leaving a big yellow stain, and said, "Sorry, Jack, but you're on your own with that. Let's just say I owe you a pastrami sandwich."

17.

A Night at the Races

So it was back to the Left Coast, back to Santa Monica, back to the Wyndham Hotel. If Libby Leverton's story was to be believed, Scooter Lowry needed money and he thought he would inherit some from Henry. To do that, he needed to stop his uncle from giving it all away.

I had to find out if Scooter had a financial problem, and, if he did, if it was serious enough to cause him to commit murder.

My computer hacker, Lucy Gates, had been unable to discover Scooter's problem, maybe because Scooter and his pal Stanley would talk about it in person, no texts, e-mails, or phone conversations, so I'd have to rely upon the ages-old detecting technique: shoe leather. Boots on the ground. A full-out infantry assault. Woody Allen said, "Showing up is 80 percent of life." I had to show up.

Again.

You can't do surveillance while driving a car like a Dodge Charger GT, so I rented a generic tan Nissan sedan at LAX. A car so ordinary that you might not notice it if it was parked in your living room. The allegedly half-hour or so drive north along Pacific Coast Highway to Santa Monica took twice as long due to a gapers' block caused by a multi-car pileup in the southbound lanes, headed the other way from me. Gapers' blocks usually drive me absolutely batty. *Why slow down when there is no problem in your lanes? Haven't you ever seen an accident before, people?* But it was not a problem this time, because one of the Nissan's radio tuning buttons was set to KJAZZ FM, a very good LA jazz and blues station. Which would have been even better if the car had a good audio system, but renters can't be choosers.

I checked into the Wyndham, had lunch at Izzy's Deli on Wilshire Boulevard recommended by the desk clerk. I got a large coffee and three glazed doughnuts to go, then motored over to Scooter's house and parked on the street to begin my surveillance.

It was late afternoon, California time. I didn't know if Scooter was at home. I'd considered wearing a disguise, like Elizabeth and Philip Jennings in the TV show *The Americans*, but decided that Scooter had only met me that one time at Starbucks and wouldn't be expecting to see me again. I didn't know how in the world anyone was ever fooled by the Jennings's disguises, which consisted of cheesy wigs, nerdy glasses, and sometimes, hats. They still looked like themselves, wearing wigs, glasses, and hats. You'd think that the makeup people could have done better, given that they'd made Gary Oldman look so much like Winston Churchill that he could have fooled Hitler, up close.

At six thirty, having been sustained by KJAZZ and the coffee and doughnuts, I saw Scooter come out of his house, go into the detached garage, and back out in a beautifully restored Ford Woody Wagon, probably early 1950s, with a roof rack suitable for transporting a surfboard. Think Beach Boys' "Surfin' Safari." If Scooter went down for murder, maybe I could buy that cherry Woody at a police auction. Marisa would love it.

I followed the Woody at an appropriate distance as Scooter drove across town and parked in a lot at a one-story, green cinderblock building with a neon sign identifying it as Stanley's Gym which, I'd learned, Scooter had purchased for his friend. Scooter went into the gym. I parked on the other side of the street, down a ways, and waited. Scooter didn't look like he lifted anything heavier than a beer mug, so I assumed he was at the gym to see Stanley and would be out before too long.

Which he was, just minutes later, along with Stanley. They got into Scooter's Woody. I pulled out and followed them toward the beach until they arrived at The Misfit Restaurant + Bar and parked in front.

I pulled into the beach lot across the street and debated whether or not to go into the bar to see what they were doing. Just having a drink? Or meeting with a loan shark who had Scooter by the short hairs?

They came out of the bar twenty minutes later. I followed them to the 10 Freeway entrance ramp, on the 10 to the 405, then to an exit for a town called Cypress. Heavy traffic all the way. It took so long that I needed a shave when we arrived. I didn't know why Californians called their expressways "freeways." Just to be different, I guessed. Surely, we'd passed a lot of bars along the way, so why the long drive in traffic?

I found out when we arrived at the Los Alamitos Race Course. I followed Scooter and Stanley into the large parking lot, stopping to pay the five-dollar fee to an attendant in a booth, and took a space one row over from Scooter's. I decided I'd follow them inside. If Scooter had a murderous money problem, betting on the ponies could be the reason.

I stayed back as Scooter and Stanley headed toward the track building. A sign advertised daytime thoroughbred racing and nighttime quarter horse racing. It was dark, so we'd see the quarter horses. I didn't know one equine from another. I'd watched the movie *Secretariat* while at home recovering from one of my gunshot wounds and found it to be very moving. At one point, I shouted out, "Let the big horse run!" Probably the aftereffect of the anesthesia.

I mingled with the crowd as we entered the building, paying another five bucks for clubhouse admission, because I'd seen Scooter and Stanley walking toward an elevator marked "To Clubhouse." I hadn't even placed a bet yet and I was already ten bucks down. That's why I don't gamble.

They got into the elevator along with a group of other people. I waited for the next one, rode it up, got out, and spotted them in a large, open club room, seated at a high-top table next to a wall of windows overlooking the track. A waitress arrived, spoke with them, walked away, and soon returned with two tall mugs of foamy beer. They looked good to me. Day at a time. I hung back beside the bar, out of sight. They sipped their beers. A man's voice over a loudspeaker announced that it was ten minutes to post time, so place your bets.

There were four betting windows on the other side of the bar from me. Scooter and Stanley went to the windows, waited in line, then walked back to their table holding paper betting receipts.

The race began. Secretariat wasn't entered. Even if the big horse was alive and in California, I did know from the movie that he was a thoroughbred, not a quarter horse. A horse named Sunny Side Up won by a length. It was apparent that Scooter and Stanley hadn't bet on him, or her, to win, place, or show, because they ripped their receipts in half and dropped them onto the floor. Littering, but track officials were unlikely to hassle customers who paid their salaries, and then some.

Nine races and three more beers later, the boys left the building, all of their receipts ripped in half and dropped onto the floor. I went over and picked up the receipts. All were twenty-dollar win bets. They'd each dropped two hundred simoleons. Not their lucky night. If Scooter had a serious betting jones, wagering on horses at the track and on sports, political elections, and whether or not Punxsutawney Phil would see his shadow, with a bookie, could land him in a financial jam.

I tailed Scooter for three more days. He surfed, showing considerable skill I could see from the beach, hit the bars, visited Stanley's Gym, got a haircut, went for a spin on his dirt bike, and one night took a lovely young woman to dinner at a fancy restaurant called the Sea Salt Fish Grill.

I waited in the parking lot, dining on two cheeseburgers, fries, and a strawberry shake from a Sonic Drive-In I'd passed. I was upset to see on the drive-thru menu that one of my all-time favorite burger joints now offered vegetarian burgers.

It was three A.M. when I was awakened by a pounding on my hotel room door. Seal Team 6? *Stand down, bin Laden's not here, boys. Have you tried Pakistan, back in 2011?*

I took my Glock from my suitcase, which I could fly with because I had police credentials, jacked a round into the chamber, and said, with as much menace in my voice as I could muster: "Who's there?"

"Would you believe room service?" a voice answered that sounded like Scooter's, if I remembered correctly.

I opened the door to find Scooter and Stanley standing in the hallway, no weapons in their hands, so I invited them in.

"Why have you been following me?" Scooter asked.

"Was I that obvious?"

"You'll recall that Stanley was a skip tracer," Scooter told me.

Which made me feel a bit better about my tradecraft skills.

"I'll ask again, why are you following me?" Scooter said.

I had a gun and they didn't, so I decided to level with them.

"I talked to your cuz, Libby Leverton. She told me about that family meeting at Alan Dumont's law firm in Washington. Libby, June Dumont, Alan, and you were there, she said. All of you assumed at that time you were your rich Uncle Henry's only heirs. Libby said a private detective hired by Alan reported that Henry was giving away large amounts of money, and that you mentioned that it would be a shame, meaning not a shame, if Henry had an accident before he squandered all of his wealth. Libby also told me about the idea to petition for an Illinois probate court proceeding seeking to have Henry declared mentally incompetent, and June appointed as his guardian. The problem being that it could take nearly a year for a decision, during which time Henry would keep spending. She said that you seemed especially upset by that. That made me wonder if you decided to rub out Henry because you have a financial problem and needed inheritance cash."

"Rub out" being an old-time crime-noir term I thought was kind of cool.

Scooter asked, "Did Libby mention that her husband, Stewart, was also at the meeting?"

"She did not," I told him.

"It was Alan's idea to bring the probate court action," Scooter said. "Thinking like a lawyer, and everyone thought it was a good idea except for the timing. I was just blowing smoke, like I do. However, Stewart seemed downright distraught. Maybe he's the one with money problems. Developers go broke all the time. He should be at the top of your suspect list, not me."

I tended to believe him. That would explain why Libby had taken the trouble to come to Fort Myers Beach, all the way from Boston, to tell me about Scooter's comments at that family meeting at the law firm, in order to divert my attention from herself and her husband. It worked.

I was curious about something, and asked Scooter: "Why are you here at this hour of the morning? The witching hour."

"The witching what?"

"Never mind that part."

"Ah, we were out having a few beers," Scooter said. "Your hotel was on the way home, so we decided to stop by instead of coming back in the morning. Didn't want to miss you."

As they were leaving, I said, "That's a very nice Woody you have, Scooter. A real classic."

Sadly, there would be no police auction.

"Thanks," he said. "It was a twenty-first birthday gift from my father. He was a very successful businessman. He took care of me for life. Yes, I do a little gambling, and some partying, and I like nice cars, and cycle racing, and I don't have a job per se, but I use my father's financial advisor to manage my portfolio, and I'm doing just fine."

"And the gym makes a profit, if he ever needs any dough, which he doesn't," Stanley added.

I nodded, they left, and I went back to sleep.

I had a nine thirty A.M. flight from LAX to Boston. I was racking up enough air-mile points on this case to earn a trip on Elon Musk's SpaceX rocket to Mars. Or at least a set of steak knives. After my chat with Scooter, I now believed Stewart Leverton was my man and that Libby was his partner in crime. If he wasn't, I was out of suspects.

I had coffee, OJ, pancakes, and bacon for breakfast at Izzy's, then checked out of the hotel and drove to the airport to catch a flight to Boston. I stopped in a gift shop in the terminal to buy a book to help pass the time on the long flight. They had three of Bill Stevens's Jack Stoney books. Pass on those, I lived them. I selected the latest in the Prey series by John Sandford. His detective, Lucas Davenport, has a high close rate. Not as high as Stoney (and me), but still impressive.

18.

Officer Needs Assistance

Coincidentally, I had the same driver that I did for my last cab ride from Logan airport into Boston. The driver recognized me, too, and asked, "Say, did you get scrod your last time here?"

I checked into the Hyatt Regency. I put my overnight bag in my room and discovered, wonder of wonders, that it was dinner time. It was unseasonably warm, the daylight faded into dusk, so I took a walk, directed by a city map I got from the desk clerk, in search of vittles. After a while, I came upon the historic Faneuil Hall Marketplace. In Boston, everything is historic, or built to look that way.

Lots of restaurants to choose from, but a sign on the Quincy Market building caught my eye, advertising Fat Thomas's Tavern, established in 1827. I hoped the food was fresher than that. I went inside, found myself in the restaurant's bar, and was told by the bartender to take the stairway to the dining room on the second floor.

The cavernous dining room was full of people sitting side by side at long picnic tables. I found an open section of bench between a middle-aged man in a suit and a young woman wearing a Boston Police Department uniform. A waitress came over, put a menu on the table in front of me, filled my water glass, and said, "Whenever you're ready, I'll take your order. And hurry it up, I ain't got all day."

She stood there with her arms folded, staring at me and tapping her foot. She looked to be in her fifties, and was thin, with an angular face and short, curly brown hair. The name tag on her uniform said Sally.

The lady cop smiled at me and said, sotto voce, "The waitresses here are notoriously rude. It's part of the charm of the place."

Sally could hear that but pretended not to. She gave me one last glare and went off to harass other patrons.

I scanned the menu and noticed that they spelled scrod as "schrod." Must be the way they spelled it in 1827. The businessman was eating a massive piece of rare prime rib, swimming in au jus, overflowing his plate.

The lady cop said, "Prime rib is the specialty here, along with the Yankee pot roast, clam chowder, Boston baked beans, and Indian pudding." She was eating a fried clam roll.

"Thanks for the tip," I told her. "It's my first time here."

"You had sort of a deer-in-the-headlights look," she said. "Where you from?"

"Chicago originally. Florida now."

Sally the waitress came back and said, "*Now* do you know what you want?"

"I'll have the chicken pot pie," I told her.

She gave me a disapproving look, and said, "The prime rib's better, buster, and so's the pot roast, but some people can't be helped," and left me to wallow in my ignorance.

"My name's Millie," the lady cop said. "My parents named me Millicent, if you can believe that, after one of my aunts, who always said she hated her name. She was named after her mother, who also hated her name. Same with my grandmother. Gotta keep that nomenclature of hate going down through the generations, I guess."

"My name's Jack Starkey," I said.

"You here on business or pleasure, Jack?"

Her name tag said Ryan. She wore corporal's stripes. Millie Ryan was a fellow traveler, so I said, "Business. Police business."

"An interesting case?" she asked me.

"About as interesting as it gets," I said.

She looked at me expectantly, like my cat, Joe, did when he wanted to be fed.

Sally arrived with my chicken pot pie, which she dropped in front of me with a harrumph.

"Have you been here since 1827, Sally?" I asked her.

She laughed, punched me on the arm, and said: "Good for you, darlin'. I like bein' sassed back."

She went off and I felt like a Fat Thomas's Tavern regular.

"You were saying it was an interesting case," Millie reminded me when Sally was gone.

I thought about it for a while, then I told her the whole story. When I finished the narrative, and the chicken pot pie, Millie said, "Wowie. When I grow up, I want to be a detective, just like you."

"Let's hope you can do better," I told her, meaning it.

"If you're planning on checking in with the department . . ."

"I am," I told her. Tom Sullivan had already called his Boston counterpart to clear the way.

"I recommend hooking up with a homicide detective named Danny O'Rourke," Millie told me.

As she had? I wondered.

"And if you need a driver, ask for me," she added.

"Definitely," I told her.

We both paid our checks to my new pal Sally. I left a 30 percent tip to make up for my ordering ineptitude. Then we walked downstairs and outside. Millie's radio squawked. She pushed a button on the microphone hanging on her right shoulder and said, "Ryan."

A female dispatcher's voice said: "Got a Code Three at One Ten Kilby Street."

"On the way," Millie told her.

She looked at me. "That's nearby. Someone needs help. Good to meet you, Jack."

"Be careful out there," I told her.

She winked at me and hurried off. I wondered if she was too young to catch the reference.

I walked back to the Hyatt Regency, watched the Bruins play the Red Wings on TV, switched to a movie, *Road House*, which I'd seen countless times, a cinematic classic, then slept soundly.

The next morning, I had breakfast in the hotel coffee shop and called the Boston Police Department, a phone number I'd entered into my contacts list. A woman answered by saying, "Boston Police Department. With whom do you wish to speak?"

With *whom* do I wish to speak? Correct grammar. Another moonlighting Harvard student?

"Please put me through to Detective Danny O'Rourke in homicide," I said.

"What is this regarding?"

Why does every receptionist want to know what my call is regarding? Do I have the voice of a time-wasting crank?

"It's a Code Forty-Four," I said.

"I'm not familiar with that code," she said.

"Officer needs assistance."

"That's a Ten Thirteen."

"Let's not get bogged down numerically," I said. "I'm a police officer from Florida and I need Detective O'Rourke's assistance."

"Wait one," she said.

After more than one, a voice said, "O'Rourke."

A man of few words.

"This is Jack Starkey," I said. "I'm a detective with the Naples, Florida, Police Department. I'm in Boston on a case. Your Chief Summerfield knows about it."

"Summerfield told you to call me?"

"No, it was one of your officers. Corporal Millie Ryan."

"How do you know my niece?" he asked.

Niece. Shame on me for thinking otherwise.

"We met last night at Fat Thomas's Tavern," I explained.

"You have the prime rib?"

"The chicken pot pie."

"Like the tourist that you are. So what's up, Detective Starkey?"

"Do you have any time to get together today?" I asked him.

"I'm jammed up. But I can do dinner. Divorced guys can always do dinner."

"I hear you."

"You like Italian food?" he asked me.

"Be a fool not to," I answered.

"Let's say seven at Carmelina's, 307 Hanover Street in the North End. No chicken pot pie, but they have spaghetti carbonara that'll make you wish you lived here."

"See, that's why I need your help," I told him.

"Seven o'clock," he said, and ended the call.

I went back to my room with a day to kill before dinner. Boston was a town with many sights to see. I checked the location of the Boston Common on my city map from the hotel. I'd read in a guidebook in my room that, until 1817, an ancient elm on the land was used for public hangings. I wondered if the elm was still there and if I could use it to threaten Stewart Leverton into confessing his many sins of commission and omission. I'd ask him to meet me at the tree and show up with a rope and a few questions.

Boston Common was nearby, so I walked over, saw a number of elm trees, all suitable for necktie parties, sat on a park bench near an old man who was tossing peanuts from a bag to squirrels, and called Marisa, Sam, and Tom Sullivan. Marisa and Sam were doing fine. Sullivan said, "Good idea to hook up with a local detective. What plan are you on now?"

"Either D or E. After a while, they all blur together."

"I grew up in Quincy," Sullivan said. "I highly recommend you eat at Fat Thomas's Tavern at least once."

"I had dinner there last night," I said.

"What'd you have?"

"The prime rib," I told him.

I passed the rest of the day strolling around the city, following my map, which highlighted Boston locations tourists should visit. I found the Downtown Freedom Trail and followed it easily because it was well marked, passing the Massachusetts State House, the Park Street Church, the Old South Meeting House, the Old Corner Bookstore, and other attractions. The common theme was that everything was very old, and therefore important.

The highlight of my tour was lunch at the Union Oyster House, which was located in a redbrick building at 41 Union Street. A historical marker out front declared that the place, opened in 1826, was the oldest continuously operating restaurant in America. I recalled that Fat Thomas's Tavern opened a year later, causing it to be considered a relative newcomer to the Boston restaurant scene.

Inside, the cozy little place was all dark wood and brass and full with a convivial lunch crowd savoring Ye Olde Yankee fare. I noticed that there actually was a Ye Olde Gift Shop inside. Maybe I'd get a Ye Olde scented candle for Marisa and a Ye Olde wind chime to drive Joe batty.

I sat at the curved bar near the live-lobster tank, scanned the menu, and told the bartender I wanted the clams casino for openers and then, what the hell, the Boston Scrod, which was a baked cod fillet topped with seasoned bread crumbs, the bartender explained when I asked. Given the atmosphere of the place, I felt like I should also ask for a seafaring drink like a grog or hot buttered rum, but I got a diet root beer instead.

The scrod was yummy. Definitely not a joke.

19.

Saint Michael the Archangel

That night, central casting sent me a Boston homicide detective named Danny O'Rourke. I spotted him easily among the bar patrons at Carmelina's: a big, beefy guy with the build of a Boston College lineman which, I found out later, he had been. He was spiffy in a houndstooth sport coat. I could see the print of a gun in a shoulder holster under it. He had that whiter-than-white Irish skin, with red spider veins on his nose and cheeks. This wasn't the first bar Danny O'Rourke had been in.

I walked over and said, "Detective O'Rourke, I'm Jack Starkey."

"My niece describe me?"

"No. You kind of stand out. Either a cop, or a well-dressed iron worker."

I could tell he liked that.

"Join me in a Tullamore Dew?" he asked.

"Thanks, but I'm off the hard stuff," I told him.

"Day at a time."

"That's the program."

"I'm thinking about cutting back to a gallon a week," he said. "Don't want it to become a problem."

He finished his drink and led us to a table along the back wall. He took the seat against the wall, facing outward. Good tradecraft. Easy to spot a bad guy coming at him.

A waiter in his late sixties or early seventies appeared and said, "Daniel, my boy. It's been awhile."

O'Rourke grinned and said, "Tommaso, meet Jack Starkey from Florida."

Tommaso nodded at me and asked Danny, "He a detective too? He's got the look."

"Just here to see the sights," I told him.

"Right," he said. "Just seeing the sights. Can I get you boys a drink?"

"The usual for me," O'Rourke said. "And a grape Kool-Aid for him."

"Diet root beer if you have it," I said.

"We do," Tommaso said. "Don't sell much of it though."

He went to get our drinks, mine apparently being a disgrace to my Irish heritage.

"Your chief called my chief who talked to the lieutenant in charge of our Homicide Unit who gave me an overview of why you're here," O'Rourke said. "Fill me in on the details."

For the second time since arriving in Boston, I did that. During the telling, Tommaso arrived with our drinks and took our dinner order, the spaghetti carbonara for both of us. Having been burned at Fat Thomas's Tavern, I now knew to order one of the house specialties.

When I finished my tale, long story long, and we were well into the carbonara, which was excellent, O'Rourke said, "We may need to call in Saint Michael from the bench for this one."

I knew exactly who that was: Saint Michael the Archangel, patron saint of police officers. My mother gave me his medal when I graduated from the Chicago Police Academy. I wore it on a chain around my neck under my tee shirt from that day until I retired. I had that medal at home in a drawer. It was a silver shield with the raised figure of Saint Michael, wings and all, holding a broadsword with its point in the belly of a serpent-like figure at his feet and the words "Saint Michael Protect Us" around the outer edge.

"Now that's the second reason I need your help," I said. "You know how to put a team together."

Tommaso brought us each an espresso and cannoli, without being asked. We lingered over dessert as we talked about how to bring down Stewart Leverton, and maybe Libby, too, for murder.

"I've heard of Leverton," O'Rourke said. "He's a major commercial real estate developer who's often in court for not paying his subs and for thinking that building and zoning laws are guidelines, not absolute rules."

"That's what Scooter Lowry told me," I said.

O'Rourke said, "You can come to police headquarters, borrow a desk, and use a computer to get into our database if you want."

"Thanks," I told him. "I'll do that."

More than using a desk and computer, I was eager to breathe in the atmosphere of a big-time law-enforcement operation again.

As we finished dessert, O'Rourke asked, "How would Detective Jack Stoney handle this case?"

I smiled. "You've done your homework about me."

"I'm actually a fan of the books," he said. "Stoney's a hell of a homicide cop."

"I could use his help right now," I said.

"Most days, I could too."

I asked him, "You know about that hanging oak in Boston Common?"

He smiled. "Do I ever. O'Rourke family legend has it that a distant relative, who was a horse thief, met his untimely end on that very tree. An Irish family that doesn't have a horse thief or two, some alcoholics, politicians, cops, and maybe a poet, isn't very interesting."

20.

The Cow Paths of Boston

The next morning, to keep up with Danny O'Rourke, in the sartorial sense, I dressed in an open-collar blue shirt, navy blazer, tan slacks, and cordovan loafers, found a restaurant near the hotel called The Shamrock, had an enjoyable breakfast of baking powder biscuits with sausage gravy, and good coffee, and told a cabbie to deliver me to Boston Police Headquarters at One Schroeder Plaza, the address on O'Rourke's business card.

We pulled up in front of a glass-and-concrete mid-rise building, modern, not "olde." I went inside and told the receptionist who I was meeting. She directed me to an elevator that took me to the Homicide Unit on the third floor.

I strolled around the big room and found O'Rourke in a cubicle, talking on the phone. He nodded at me, ended the call, and said, "I'd like you to meet Lieutenant Halloran."

I followed him across the room to an office with an open door. He knocked on the door jamb and we entered. A tall, thin man in his forties, it looked, stood up from his desk chair, and said, "Detective Starkey, I presume," echoing Henry Morton Stanley's greeting to Dr. David Livingstone after tracking him down in Africa. Or maybe that was just how Halloran greeted everyone.

"I'm Roger Halloran," he told me. "Glad to have you visit us."

We shook hands and I said, "I appreciate your hospitality, Lieutenant. And Detective O'Rourke's help. I'll try not to take too much of his time."

"Danny told me about your case," he said. "He's one of our best. Good hunting."

As I followed O'Rourke to his cubicle, he said, "Halloran didn't mean *one* of our best, he meant our *best*. He didn't want to embarrass me."

When we got back to his cubicle, he indicated the one next to his and said, "You can use this one. Steve Bancroft's at home trying to pass a kidney stone."

"Ouch."

"Use that computer to access our system," he told me. "The password's fightingirish, one word, lowercase. The LT's a Notre Dame grad. I've arranged for you to use a car. Have at it and let me know what you need."

"Where's the coffee?" I asked him.

He pointed to a back corner of the room. "Over there, next to the bathrooms." As if he could read my mind, he added, "You want doughnuts, get here early."

O'Rourke sat at his desk and I made my way to the coffee room. As advertised, a big Dunkin' Donuts box with the top open held only crumbs. Instead of the traditional Bunn coffee maker holding burned, acidic liquid, there was a restaurant-grade espresso machine, and a refrigerator, which implied good coffee, and real milk, not that awful powdered coffee creamer. Score points for the Boston PD.

I was staring at the espresso machine, with all its bells and whistles, valves and chrome spouts, without the faintest idea about how to get a cup of coffee out of it when a woman of about forty came in, looked at me, and said, "I'm Alison. Call me Al. Can I be of assistance?"

A gold detective's shield in a black leather case was clipped to the waistband of her slacks. "I'm Jack," I responded. "And you sure can. I didn't go to MIT, but I'd like a cup of coffee."

She smiled. "Done and done. Would you like espresso, cappuccino, a latte, or maybe a macchiato? I can also do a Frappuccino or herbal tea."

"I'm more in the mood for an actual cup of coffee," I said sheepishly.

"Oh, you mean a Caffè Americano," she told me.

I didn't, but I was encouraged by the "Americano" part, so I said, "That'd be good, thank you."

Al fired up the machine with the skill of an engineer at the controls of a steam locomotive. Maybe she'd spent her junior year in Italy. After much whooshing and gurgling, out into a white ceramic mug with a Boston PD logo on it came what I recognized as an actual cup of coffee.

"Milk's in the fridge, sugar and sweetener in the cupboard," she told me as she began to fix one of the more complex drinks for herself.

"I take it black," I told her. "By the way, I'm Jack Starkey, a detective from Florida."

"I heard we're having a visitor," she said. "You need more coffee, come find me."

I took the mug back to Bancroft's cubicle. I sat at the desk, fired up the computer, and searched the departmental database to see if Stewart Leverton had a criminal record. As I expected, he didn't, and neither did Libby. Not yet.

I finished the coffee, took the elevator back to the lobby, and asked the receptionist where I could find the motor pool. She directed me out through a back door to the employees' parking lot. There was a booth with a middle-aged uniformed officer in it. He must have screwed something up royally to be assigned to parking lot duty. I told him that Detective O'Rourke had reserved a car for me.

He took a set of keys off a pegboard, handed them to me, and said, "Space ten. Bring it back with a full tank."

Just like Hertz, except he didn't ask if I wanted the supplemental insurance.

Space ten held a chocolate-brown Ford Taurus with black-wall tires and a whip antenna on the roof. It didn't need Boston PD markings to scream out "Police! Halt!"

I decided I'd begin Plan D, if my plan count was accurate, by cruising past the Leverton home on Beacon Hill. I entered the address of their row house on Beacon Street into Google Maps on my cell phone, fired up the Taurus's big Police Interceptor engine, and waited for the Google lady to tell me which way to go. But the only voice I heard was that of the dispatcher on the police radio. The Google lady was either on a break or she didn't do Boston.

I opened MapQuest on my cell phone and entered the Levertons' address, which produced written directions and a little map with a bold black line showing my route. I backed out of the parking space and drove onto the street. After ten minutes of trying to follow the directions through winding, crooked streets, I was not at my destination. In fact, I had no idea where I was. The street signs were in Chinese. Maybe I could find my way back to that neighborhood for dinner that night, but probably not. However, I could stop to get a carryout menu from one of the zillion Chinese restaurants and order a delivery to the Hyatt Regency.

With that in mind, I pulled over in front of Yee's Noodle House, parked at the curb, and spotted a taxi stopped across the street. I walked over and asked the driver, a man in his fifties, I thought, for directions to Beacon Hill.

He thought about that and said, "Well, that's tricky. Boston streets began as cow paths in Colonial times. It's a wonder that the cows ever found their barns. I used to drive a cab in New York. Now that's a logical street pattern. Here, it's total chaos."

I thanked the cabbie and began to walk away when he said, "I do of course know how to get to Beacon Hill. It's just that I can't articulate it."

Articulate. In Boston, everyone was either a college student or graduate, or talked like one. I had an idea: "How about if I follow you there, with your meter running?"

He shrugged and said, "Why not? A fare's a fare."

I gave him the address, and that's just what we did, arriving in less than fifteen minutes, even with heavy traffic, piece of cake, without seeing any cows. We both parked at the curb. I got out of the Taurus, walked over to the taxi, and gave the cabbie his $18.25 fare, plus a $10 tip. It occurred to me that my case had become as convoluted as the streets of Boston.

The cabbie asked, "You new to the department? Most Boston cops know their way around the city."

It was the Taurus.

"Just visiting," I answered. "But I do know enough to get the prime rib at Fat Thomas's Tavern."

He said, "I like their chicken pot pie better," and drove away.

Nice neighborhood: narrow streets with gaslights, brick sidewalks, and blocks of brick and grey-clapboard row houses, all well-maintained. The Beacon Hill Property Owners Association wouldn't let me buy one because the Starkey family came to America via Ellis Island, not Plymouth Rock.

From the sidewalk, I studied the Levertons' Federal Style row house: three stories, red brick, black door and shutters, six steps up from the street to a small front porch, and a brass plaque bolted to the wall beside the door that probably said: "George Washington, Benjamin Franklin, and Paul Revere Slept Here." Or maybe: "No Soliciting."

I walked up the steps and rang the doorbell. The brass plaque did not say "No Soliciting," a good thing because I would have had to leave. It said "1783." Like The Drunken Parrot, the Levertons' row house probably needed a new roof after all that time.

After a few minutes, no one answered the door and came out with their hands up and confessed to the murder of Henry Wilberforce. My work there was done, at least for the moment, so I went back to the Taurus.

Next stop was Stewart Leverton's office, which, I'd learned from the company's website, was in a building called Exchange Place at 53 State Street. Yeah, right. I remembered the name of the taxi company that had gotten me to Beacon Hill, called it, and gave the dispatcher the Levertons' address. The same driver showed up ten minutes later. He got out of the cab, walked over to my car, smiled, and said, "Thought we might be hearing from you again. Now where to?"

I followed the taxi to Exchange Place, paid the fare, and gave the cabbie another $10 tip. I was beginning to think of him as Tenzing Norgay, the Sherpa who guided Edmund Hillary to the summit of Mount Everest, which might have been easier to find than any destination in Boston because all you had to do was climb straight up.

I thought the cabbie got lost on the way because we passed some of the same buildings and street corners twice, but I let it go. He was, after all, a New Yorker, where the island of Manhattan was laid out in a uniform grid, with the streets running east and west, the avenues running north and south, and where the Bronx is up and the Battery's down.

Now and then, Marisa and I flew to New York, which the locals called "The City" as if there were no other, for a weekend of shopping, theater-going, and fine dining. As for the dining, she preferred restaurants with lots of stars and white tablecloths, like Per Se, Le Bernardin, and Guantanamera, where we didn't go very often because it was Cuban and Marisa's cooking was better. But sometimes she liked to see if the chef was doing anything new and noteworthy. I liked the pastrami sandwiches at Katz's Deli, the hot dogs at Nathan's Famous, and the steak sandwiches at the Lobel's stand in Yankee Stadium. For one thing, you didn't have to book a reservation at my places ten years in advance. But life was compromise. To get along, you go along. Quid pro quo. You scratch my back . . . and so forth.

I'd decided to use the same tactic with Stewart Leverton as I had with Alan Dumont. Show up unannounced at his office, get in his face, and see if he exhibited any poker-game kind of "tell," such as beginning to sob uncontrollably when I confronted him, or scream and run for it, or hold out his wrists for handcuffs. Or reach in his desk drawer for a pistol.

Another building lobby, another receptionist, another elevator up to a suite of offices, in this case, the fortieth-floor headquarters of Leverton Properties LLC.

"I'm here to see Stewart Leverton," I told the young woman behind the second receptionist desk standing between me and my prey. I paused for the standard question.

And she asked it: "May I ask what this is regarding?"

How to answer? If I said "None of your beeswax, little lady. Tell your boss to get out here now or his ass is grass," she'd sound the silent alarm and I'd be frog-marched to the street by building security.

"It's a personal matter," I told her.

She said, "I'm afraid that Mr. Leverton is gone for the day."

"Will he be in tomorrow?" I asked her.

"I'm afraid that I don't have that information," she answered.

Leverton Properties LLC needed to hire a receptionist who wasn't a scaredy-cat.

"May I tell him your name?" she asked.

"Wyatt Earp," I said, winked at her, and hightailed it out of Dodge.

Maybe his development business was slow, or Stewart Leverton was a fast worker, to leave so early during a weekday. Or maybe he was feeling ill or went home to help his wife hang new wallpaper in the dining room. Or to retrieve false passports and a stack of cash so he and Libby could take his private jet to a country without an extradition treaty with the US.

If showing up was 80 percent of life, I needed to find a way to close the gap on the remaining 20 percent.

I decided to try the Levertons' row house again, just in case Stewart had gone there from the office and I'd just missed him. If

Magellan could circumnavigate the globe without GPS, I should be able to use dead reckoning to drive back to the Levertons' row house without following my Sherpa guide again. At night, I could navigate by the stars, if I knew how to do that, which I did not: Twinkle, twinkle, little star, I have no idea who you are, or where I am.

I made it to my destination by stopping three times to ask directions, once from a woman pushing a baby stroller, once in a Walgreens, and the third time from a city worker just emerging from a manhole. He laughed and said it was easier to get there underground, but he did direct me to the Levertons' row house using surface streets.

I parked the Taurus in front of a fire hydrant. A beat cop would recognize the car as a police vehicle and not issue a ticket or call for a tow. I walked up the steps of the row house and rang the doorbell. After a few moments, a very thin older man with snow-white hair and a hooked nose, dressed in butler's garb, answered the door.

"Yes, sir?" he asked with an English accent. Central casting again.

"I was here a little while ago and no one was home," I told him.

"I'm very sorry for your inconvenience, sir, but our doorbell was broken," he explained. "The repairman was just here."

"I guess that happens when doorbells get that old," I said.

"That old, sir?"

"Installed in 1783," I said.

He smiled, getting my joke, and said, "I should imagine it's a bit newer than that."

"I'd like to speak with Mr. and Mrs. Leverton," I told him.

"I'm sorry, sir, but they are not home at present," he said.

"Do you know when they will return?"

"The mister and missus are hosting a dinner party here tonight," he said. "They should be here in a few hours. May I tell them your name?"

I didn't want to warn them that they would have an extra dinner guest, so I said, "I'm Jack Stoney. I'll catch them another time."

Jack Stoney, my alter ego. I didn't imagine that this English butler read Bill's books. Probably stuck with English classics like *David Copperfield* and *Wuthering Heights*.

I found my way back to police headquarters, stopping only two times to ask directions. Progress. One time, I asked a man in his sixties walking along a sidewalk who was, I swear, dressed like a Continental soldier. I pulled up beside him, stopped, powered down the window, and said, "Pardon me, sir. Which way are the British? I'd like to head in the opposite direction."

He laughed and said, "I'm just coming from a parade. I can assure you that the British have been thoroughly beaten and are no longer a threat to the city."

"Well, that's a relief," I said. "In that case, can you direct me to police headquarters at One Schroeder Plaza?"

"Sure can," he said, and gave me very specific directions, which I followed until I got lost.

To my good fortune, I spotted a Dunkin' Donuts at a street corner and parked in front of it, next to a fire hydrant. Dunkin' Donuts stores were as ubiquitous in Boston, the chain was founded nearby, as college students and seafood restaurants.

I went inside and bought two baker's-dozen assorted from the counter girl as a gift for the Homicide Unit. Jack Starkey, always the good guest. I walked out of the store and found a Boston police officer on a Harley-Davidson motorcycle parked behind my Taurus. He was tall, in his late twenties or early thirties, wearing a white helmet with a Boston PD logo, a black leather jacket, dark blue jodhpurs with tall black boots, and sunglasses—Ray-Bans, not Oakleys. A cool dude. In my experience, motorcycle cops did the job for the outfits, mostly.

He looked at the Taurus and asked, "You on the job or did you steal this car?"

"I borrowed it for a doughnut run," I said.

I opened one of the two boxes I was carrying, rested it on the Harley saddle, and said, "Take your pick, officer."

"Trying to bribe a police officer is a felony," he said as he selected a glazed raised. "I'll let you off this time with a warning."

"I appreciate that," I said. "Can you give me directions to your headquarters while these are still fresh? I'm not from here."

"Better follow me," he said, and turned on the Harley's siren and flashing lights. Officer Studley knew an emergency when he saw one.

I pulled into the police headquarters parking lot behind the Harley and turned into a staff-only space. The officer stopped his cycle, somehow maintaining his balance without putting a foot down, snapped a salute my way, and powered back out onto the street in search of real lawbreakers.

Just then, Corporal Millie Ryan pulled into the lot, driving a squad car with another officer in the passenger seat. I exited the Taurus, took the doughnut boxes from the back seat, and walked over to her car. Millie and her passenger got out and she said, "Hey, Jack. Is that evidence you're carrying?"

Her partner was a man with sergeant's stripes on his uniform jacket sleeves. He came around the car to provide backup, eyeing the Dunkin' boxes.

"It is, but before I check it into the property room, would you like to have a look?" I asked Millie.

"Sure, if it won't break the chain of custody," she said.

I put the boxes on the trunk of their car, opened the top box as I had for the motorcycle cop, and said, "Take your pick. I won't rat you out to Internal Affairs."

Millie selected a white frosted with sprinkles and her partner took two chocolate-coated, saying, "Rank has its privileges."

I followed them through a back door into the headquarters building that required a code to open and rode the elevator up to the Homicide Unit. I was on my way to the coffee room when a portly, forty-something man, dressed Rotary-Club style in a cranberry double-knit sport coat, stopped me, looked at the Dunkin' Donuts boxes, and said, "Whoever you are, you're always welcome here in Homicide."

I opened one of the boxes again. He picked up a powdered-sugar doughnut, examined it, put it back in the box, brushing the powder off his hands onto the floor, picked up a plain cake doughnut, gave it a slight squeeze, put it back, selected a jelly-filled, took a bite, smiled and said, "If you ever get pulled over for speeding in this city, tell 'em Tony Petrocelli says you get a free pass."

Tony walked away with his jelly doughnut. I took the two boxes, now containing twenty-one doughnuts, to the coffee room, selected a glazed raised, partly because Tony hadn't touched it, looked at the espresso machine, shrugged, and went to my cubicle, where I called Tom Sullivan in Naples, who asked, "How are you doing in the Hub City, Jack?"

I was aware of that nickname for Boston because of a piece in the *New Yorker* by John Updike, in October of 1960, about Ted Williams's last game at Fenway Park before retiring. The article was titled "Hub Fans Bid Kid Adieu." I considered that to be the finest piece of sports journalism I'd ever read. But I didn't know where that nickname for the city came from, so I asked him about it.

"It's a shortened phrase from Oliver Wendell Holmes, who wrote, Boston State-House is the hub of the solar system," Sullivan, the Quincy native, explained. "Anyway, what's up?"

I told him everything that had happened since my last update.

"So you're going to show up at the Levertons' dinner party. And you expect to be invited in to dine with them and their guests?"

"Actually, I don't know what to expect," I said. "I'm making this up as I go along."

"If you do find yourself at their dining room table, remember that the small fork is for the salad and the big spoon is for the soup."

"I'll do my best to not embarrass the Naples Police Department," I promised.

"Atta boy," he said and we ended the call.

I moved the mouse to awaken the computer from its sleep mode. There was no use trying to find out anything incriminating about the Levertons because Lucy Gates had not. I noticed an icon for *Grand Theft Auto* on the screen and played the game while waiting for the Levertons' dinnertime. I'd never played that game before, but after a few minutes I decided to download it onto my laptop at home. I was getting tired of solitaire and gin rummy.

21.

Guess Who's Coming to Dinner

I figured that drinks would be served at the Levertons' dinner party at seven, so that's when I parked the Taurus next to my favorite fire hydrant, stopping for directions only once on the way, asking a UPS driver. If I kept at it, I might even find my way to Fenway Park. I always wondered how their hot dogs compared to Wrigley Field's. Or did they only serve New England victuals? I imagined Fenway vendors walking the aisles and yelling: "Clam rolls! Getcha fried clam rolls hea! Quahogs on the half shell!"

I walked up the steps and rang that doorbell for the third time. Jeeves the butler answered as before and said, "I told Mr. Leverton you were here earlier, sir. He said that if you returned you should call his secretary at his office and make an appointment to see him there."

"Do they serve cocktails and hors d'oeuvres at his office?" I asked. "I especially like pigs-in-a-blanket."

"I expect not," Jeeves answered.

"Then I'd prefer to see him now."

"Just a moment," he said, and closed the door. It never reopened.

I called the Levertons' home number on my cell phone.

"The Leverton residence," my old friend Jeeves said when he answered.

"Stewart Leverton," I said.

"Whom may I say is calling?"

"Tell him it's John Updike. I'd like to write a piece about the dinner party for the *New Yorker*."

"Just a moment, Mr. Updike," he said. If I'd said I was Charles Dickens, he would have seen through the ruse.

After more than just a moment, Stewart came on the line and said, "John Updike is deceased. Who is this really?"

"Would you believe Oliver Wendell Holmes?" I asked him.

"Also dead. Before you try again, I'm going to hang up and block your number," he said with great annoyance in his voice.

As they said at the Department of Homeland Security, it was a credible threat, so I said, "I am in fact the police. We believe in anticipatory service."

Silence on the line.

The door opened and Stewart Leverton, dressed impeccably in a blue blazer, white shirt with a paisley ascot, and pink slacks said, "If you really are a policeman, and you do have that low-rent look, you might as well come in. We can talk in my study."

Note to self: When trying to crash a high-rent dinner party, always wear an ascot.

Stewart Leverton was a handsome man of medium height, with dark hair greying at the temples. He was wearing rimless glasses. He had a thin white scar running along his right cheek. A dueling scar? Is that how Boston real estate developers settled disputes among themselves?

He opened the door wider and stepped aside. I entered and heard the sound of jovial conviviality coming from another room. I wondered if his hit man was in attendance and was schooled in the proper use of cutlery. At least knives, obviously.

"This way," Leverton said.

I followed him down a hallway and into his study. The decor was what one would expect in a 1783 row house owned by a successful, or maybe previously successful, businessman: knotty pine paneling, an oak floor covered with an oriental rug, a vanity wall hung with photos of Leverton and what must be a panoply of VIPs, none of them Ted Williams. Stewart didn't play in that league but I did recognize him with a fellow developer, Donald Trump. Leverton and Trump were standing together on a job site, each with a hand on a silver shovel, ready to turn over the first scoop of dirt before the heavy equipment arrived.

He didn't ask if I wanted a drink or tell me to take a seat. Clearly I wasn't going to be there that long. He cut me a look that could have melted a subcontractor's heart and asked, "Now who exactly are you and what do you want?"

"I'm Detective Jack Starkey of the Naples, Florida, Police Department," I told him. "I'm investigating the murder of your wife's uncle, Henry Wilberforce."

"That crime took place in Florida?"

"Yes, that's correct."

"In that case, you have no authority here, Detective," Leverton said. "You are no more than a tourist."

"There's certainly a lot to see in your city," I replied. "I especially like the prime rib at Fat Thomas's Tavern, not to mention the spaghetti carbonara at a little Italian place in the North End whose name escapes me. However, I'm here investigating Mr. Wilberforce's murder with the knowledge and permission of Boston Police Chief Anton Summerfield. I would like to have a discussion with you and your wife about that murder."

"And you think that this social gathering at my home is the appropriate time and place for that discussion?" he asked.

"I'm not sure I can find my way to your office again," I said. "I'm lucky to be here."

He glared at me and said, "Just a moment."

But I was wise to that dodge and said, "That's fine, but after any more than a moment, I'm joining the cocktail party."

He left the study and, not wanting someone who'd obviously gone to a public high school to mingle with his high-class pals, he returned right away, accompanied by a man who said, "I am Mr. Leverton's attorney, Detective Starkey. I assume that you do not have a search warrant and that you are not here to arrest my client, even if you had the authority to do so in Boston, which you do not."

Leverton's lawyer was holding a glass, crystal no doubt, containing three fingers of a rich brown liquid, no ice. It would be a crime to add ice to what was most likely a thousand-year-old single-malt scotch. I could smell the earthy aroma of peat bogs. When I entertained aboard *Phoenix,* I served drinks to guests in a matched set of Welch's Grape Jelly glasses. They worked just fine.

"All that is correct," I told the mouthpiece. "I don't have a search warrant and I am not here to arrest Mr. Leverton, only to talk to him and his wife about a murder they may have knowledge of."

I was tempted to ask if he'd read Shakespeare's *Henry VI, Part 2* containing the line, "The first thing we do, let's kill all the lawyers." Another tip of the hat to my good Jesuit education. But I did not want to get off on the wrong foot with him.

"In that case," he told me, "you need to leave immediately."

The "or else" was implied. Maybe Stewart Leverton's hit man really was present and would come into the study holding a martini in one hand and a .22-caliber pistol with a suppressor on the barrel in the other, take a sip of his drink, and then ventilate my head.

"I can do that," I said. "And my next step will be to have a Florida court issue subpoenas to the Levertons to come to Naples for depositions."

He looked at Leverton. They stepped into the hall, closed the study door, and came back in a few minutes.

"You realize that their aforementioned depositions could just as easily be taken here," he told me. "I can petition the court for that."

Aforementioned. Harvard Law, no doubt, where they probably wore black robes and powdered wigs during moot court sessions.

He continued, "However, in order to avoid that formality, and in the spirit of full cooperation with your investigation, Mr. Leverton agrees to meet with you in my office at a mutually convenient time."

He reached into the inside breast pocket of his blazer, came out with a monogrammed gold case, opened it, and handed me his business card, which was made of a rich cream-colored stock as thick as a piece of Sheetrock. The card identified him as Worthington Dewey III of the firm Dewey, Cheatum, and Howe. Not really, but it amused me to think so.

"Works for me," I said, and put the card into my pocket.

Our business concluded, Leverton and his lawyer walked out of the study. I assumed they wanted me to follow them, which I did, down the hallway and back to the foyer. Jeeves was on station to open the front door and close it behind me, a bit harder than necessary, I thought.

Assuming that I'd still be hungry after crashing the Levertons' party, I'd arranged to meet Danny O'Rourke for dinner. This time, he chose a place called Paddy O'Doul's Pub. I'd asked him if they had good cell phone reception. He said yes, they did, why?

"Because, if Paddy's is what it sounds like, I'll have to call my AA sponsor from there."

He said, "I hear you. The corned beef and cabbage is intoxicating enough."

And so it was.

O'Rourke had given me excellent directions to the pub. "But don't ask me how to get to the Boston Opera House," he added.

When I arrived, O'Rourke was seated in a red-leather booth with a black-and-white checked tablecloth. "Whiskey in the Jar," a song by The Dubliners, was playing on the sound system, and more than a few of the patrons were singing along in full-throated voices, more enthusiastic than on key.

There were Irish pub kits you could buy, have shipped to your location, and constructed. But Paddy O'Doul's was obviously the real deal, built after 1783, I'd say, but old enough to reek of authenticity as well as stale beer, and cigarette and cigar smoke. Sawdust on the worn wooden floors. Brass spittoons, which you didn't see much of anymore.

"You should feel right at home here, Jack," Danny said. "Being Irish Catholic and all."

"Oh yeah," I told him. "I have been in a few Irish pubs over the years."

And that's when we both ordered the house specialty and talked some more about my case.

"If this was Chicago," O'Rourke said, "we'd grab Leverton off the street, stuff him in the trunk of our car, take him to an abandoned warehouse, and chat with him using enhanced interrogation techniques."

Now the song was "Molly Malone." A brawny fellow with a full red beard, wearing the attire of a construction worker, was standing on the bar, leading the chorus.

"Things like that did happen," I said. "A local station house on the South Side, Homan Square, was nicknamed The House of Screams. I was aware of it, we all were, but I never took part. You could get someone to confess to anything, including the JFK assassination, by putting his balls in a vise, but it rarely held up in court."

"There's a story about the old days in Boston," he told me. "There was a detective, skinny little guy, who could really hold his liquor. He'd come into an interrogation room with two glasses and a bottle of Jameson Irish Whiskey."

"I'm familiar with the brand," I said. "One of my old friends."

"So our detective and the suspect would drink together until the suspect was all but unconscious," O'Rourke continued. "Then the detective would have the alleged bad guy sign a document. It was a previously prepared confession, but the suspect was told it was something else. A receipt for the return of his personal effects, whatever."

"And that worked?"

"The story is probably apocryphal. But stories about coaxing out a confession using the Boston telephone directory as a motivational tool probably are true. Of course, those were the good old days."

We finished dinner. The City of Naples picked up the check. Tom Sullivan wouldn't mind because I was getting free rent in O'Rourke's Homicide Unit.

"Good hunting tomorrow," Danny O'Rourke said as we walked outside toward our cars.

22.

Shakespeare Was Right

The next morning, I called the office of Stewart Leverton's attorney. His name was Gilbert Norquist, not Worthington Dewey III, and his law firm was Norquist, Harvey & Sommerfield, not Dewey, Cheatum & Howe. A distinction without a difference.

After telling the receptionist what my call was regarding, she transferred me to his assistant and I made an appointment to see him at two o'clock that afternoon. He'd notify Leverton about the meeting, I assumed. I'd packed my exercise gear. I killed time by taking an easy run around the city, my grey Loyola baseball sweatshirt and sweatpants keeping me warm enough. Boston's Ye Olde streets were easier to navigate on foot.

After about fifteen minutes, I found myself at the Charles River watching collegiate rowing crews having a morning workout. No ice on the river, but a winter row was not my cup of tea. We did not have crew at Loyola. Based upon what I was watching, I would have chosen the Men's Ultimate Frisbee Club, which we did have, because Frisbee clearly required less aerobic conditioning, as did my sport, baseball.

I continued my run, finding my way back to the Hyatt Regency without having left a trail of bread crumbs, which pigeons would have eaten anyway, took a shower, and dressed in attire suitable for a visit to a white-shoe law firm, meaning I wore socks.

I had lunch at Mike's City Diner on nearby Washington Street, recommended by the hotel desk clerk, then drove to the law firm's building on New Sudbury Street, directed by the Google Maps lady, who'd finally found her voice. Maybe she'd been overwhelmed at first by the challenge of finding her way around the city and needed a reboot.

I parked at the curb in a loading zone, went inside the building, and rode the elevator to the twentieth floor of the thirty-story tower. Maybe, if the partners of Norquist, Harvey & Sommerfield raised their hourly billing rates, they could afford a higher floor.

Without waiting for the receptionist to ask what my presence in her lobby was regarding, I told her who I wanted to see, and why. She spoke quietly on her phone and then told me, "Mr. Norquist will see you momentarily. May I get you something to drink? We have coffee, tea, hot and iced, soft drinks, and water."

"No, but do you have a Boston telephone directory?" I asked. "The printed kind? White or Yellow Pages, whichever is thicker."

She looked confused, then recovered her poise and said, "Yes, I do. Shall I get one for you? We keep them in the stockroom."

"Hold onto it for now," I said. "I'll let you know if I need it."

After a while, she answered a call and told me to follow her to the conference room. When I got there, Stewart Leverton and Gilbert Norquist were seated near one another at one end of a long conference table. One measure of an enterprise's success apparently was the length of its conference table. The mine's-longer-than-yours syndrome.

Leverton and Norquist, who were talking, looked up at me but didn't stand when I entered. Maybe Leverton was afraid that, if he offered a handshake, I'd slap cuffs on his wrists. I took a chair without being invited to do so. I thought they taught good manners in prep school. Maybe Norquist missed that class.

Norquist said, "First, the ground rules, Detective Starkey. Mr. Leverton is willing to answer certain questions about the unfortunate demise of his wife's uncle, although, as he has stated to you previously, he has no specific knowledge of that event, nor has

Mrs. Leverton. If I feel that your questions are straying too far afield, this session will be ended. Understood?"

"Sure," I said, "as long as we agree that 'unfortunate demise' is a euphemism for murder most foul."

"We will stipulate to that," Norquist said.

I felt a rumbling in my stomach: the Mike's City Diner chili, which was nice and spicy, the way I like it. I hoped the conference room was well-ventilated, just in case.

I asked Leverton, "Do you know that Henry Wilberforce was shot in the forehead while he slept with a .22-caliber bullet in what was a professional assassination?"

"Asked and answered," Norquist said before his client could open his mouth.

"Huh. I don't recall ever asking that question, or hearing an answer," I told him. "But if your client didn't know those details, he does now."

"That's terrible," Leverton said.

Norquist gave him a look that communicated extreme displeasure that he had actually spoken to me. Bad doggie.

"Moving on," I said, "I'd like to discuss a family meeting that was held about three months ago at the Washington, DC, law firm of Alan Dumont, husband of your wife's cousin June."

Leverton didn't seem surprised that I knew about the family meeting in Washington. If this had been a Senate hearing, Norquist would have covered the microphone on the table in front of Leverton with his hand while they conferred.

"So, about that meeting," I said to Leverton. "I'm told that you also attended."

He hesitated, looked at his lawyer, who nodded permission to answer, and said, "I did, at my wife's request."

Now Norquist was allowing his client to talk. Maybe his retainer had run out.

I continued. "I'm also told that, during the meeting, it was decided to look into filing a petition in Lake County, Illinois, probate court seeking to have Mr. Wilberforce declared mentally incompetent and unable to manage his own affairs. The reason for that decision being that he was giving away large amounts of money and his sole surviving relatives, they being your wife, Libby, and her cousins, June Dumont and Scooter Lowry, were distressed by that largesse and wanted to stop it."

Largesse. I could hold my own with any Ivy Leaguer.

"That's wrong," Leverton said. "We were concerned that Henry was not able to properly take care of himself or his personal affairs. We thought it would be in his best interest to have a guardian appointed."

"The aforementioned guardian being your wife, or June, or Scooter?"

Aforementioned. Back atcha.

"Or whoever the court thought best," Leverton said.

"Speaking of Scooter," I said, "are you aware that Libby visited me in Florida and told me that she suspected Scooter was responsible for Mr. Wilberforce's murder because Scooter had financial problems and needed an inheritance?"

Leverton began to answer, but this time Norquist put his hand on his arm, looked at me, and said, "This session is ended, Detective Starkey."

I thought about getting that phone book from the stockroom or showing them the Glock I had in a belt holster at the small of my back, but decided against that because it would guarantee I would never dine at the Leverton residence.

I stood and, before leaving the conference room, looked at my watch and said, "I clocked this session at exactly seventeen minutes, Stewart. Don't let your attorney charge you for a minute more, unless it's the firm's policy to round upward, making it twenty minutes."

I saw him give the hint of a smile.

Willie Shakespeare sure was right about lawyers.

I turned to them on my way out of the room and said, "Just one more thing. Do either of you gentlemen know where I can get scrod here in Boston?"

I left without waiting for an answer.

Back in my cubicle at the Homicide Unit, I Googled Stewart's lawyer, Gilbert Norquist. No surprises: Phillips Exeter Academy prep school, Harvard undergrad, where he was on the crew and squash team, Harvard Law, clerked for a Supreme Court justice . . . Gag me with a spoon. Or maybe Norquist was one of those stolen-valor creeps and he really got his college degree from an online diploma mill, one of which had been owned by the current president of these United States, and then he went to law school on Granada. But probably not. You didn't learn to say "aforementioned" at those schools.

I realized that Stewart Leverton had not suggested that Scooter Lowry or June Dumont might have a motive for ordering the hit on Uncle Henry, or that it might be someone outside the family. Definitely significant.

Another conversation with Libby Leverton who, so far, was not lawyered up, seemed to be in order, so I called her at home. My buddy Jeeves the butler answered and, what a surprise, wanted to know what my call was regarding.

"Tell Mrs. Leverton I'm with The Mayflower Society," I said. "And we believe that one of her ancestors might have crossed the pond on that noble ship. If she can document that, we'd like her to attend our next meeting at Plymouth Rock. She'd be eligible to join our society. We have tee shirts and hats."

I'd read about The Mayflower Society in that Boston guide book in my hotel room. Sounded like a real fun group. Did they have annual conventions in Las Vegas, get liquored up, put lampshades on their heads, bet the red, and play the slots like our nation's police chiefs? Probably not. More likely, they met at the Mayflower House Museum in Plymouth, sipped tea, and gave a prize to the member who did the best British accent.

"One moment, please," Jeeves, who was now a person of interest, said.

Libby came on the line and said, "Yes?"

"It's your old pal, Jack Starkey," I said. "Do you think the Red Sox have a shot at the pennant next year?"

"I don't think we should be talking, Detective Starkey," she said. She obviously didn't follow baseball.

"But I so enjoyed our last chat, Libby," I said. "I have a few more questions."

"Stewart told me you'd been here at the house and then met with him at his lawyer's office," she said. "He said I should never talk to you again. He was quite upset about my Florida trip."

"So you didn't tell him you'd visited me? I thought he arranged your flight on his corporate jet and hired a limo."

"I arranged that trip through Stewart's executive assistant," Libby explained. "I told her the trip was confidential for a reason I could not disclose."

"She'd do that for you?"

"Yes, because I once did her a favor."

I didn't ask what that favor was because it was unimportant to my agenda. The important fact was that she hadn't told Stewart about coming to see me and naming Scooter as the likely culprit. But now he knew it because I'd spilled the Boston baked beans.

"I'm interested about why you didn't want your husband to know about your visit," I said.

"I knew he wouldn't want me meddling in your investigation."

"Because?"

"Because he'd worry that suggesting Scooter was involved in the murders could cause legal problems for us. For example, a civil suit brought by Scooter if he wasn't guilty."

That made some kind of sense. Maybe.

"I flew to California to talk to Scooter," I told her. "I don't think he was involved."

"Did you tell him what I'd said about him?" she asked.

"Yes. I felt that I had to. To explain why I was there."

"Oh, my," she said.

Oh, my, indeed.

"By the way," she said, "I already am a member of The May-flower Society."

Having set me straight, she hung up.

23.

Rube Goldberg, at Your Service

On my flight back to Fort Myers, I attempted to diagram the hot mess my case had become on a yellow legal pad I'd brought along in my overnight bag. I drew columns for all the suspects, possible motives, cities and police jurisdictions involved. I thought about having a column to list meals, but there was not enough room on the page.

Often, on those TV cop shows, the detective has all that kind of data written on a whiteboard on a wall in the squad room, plus photos of the victims and suspects pinned to a corkboard. He stares at it for long hours, rubbing his chin, and suddenly has an epiphany. He slaps his forehead. *Ah ha! Of course! Why didn't I see it before!* Then he takes his Magic Marker, draws arrows connecting the relevant boxes, and the case is solved.

My diagram looked like the sketch of a Rube Goldberg machine that would perform a simple task using an impossibly complicated mechanism: Gears were turned, chutes and ladders came into play, water rushed down a sluice, bells rang and whistles blew, a dove was released from a cage and, at the end of all that, a little flag waved.

I was in an aisle seat. I noticed that a woman in the window seat, with the middle seat open, was surreptitiously glancing at my legal pad, so I drew a smiley face saying "Hi!"

Her face reddened and she looked out the window, maybe searching for skywriting to peek at. I put the legal pad back into my briefcase and for the rest of the flight I played blackjack on my cell phone. The woman in the aisle seat studiously avoided watching. I knew it was killing her.

Back home, I checked in with Sam at the bar, visited with Tom Sullivan and Cubby Cullen, spent some quality time with Marisa, which involved walks along the beach, fine dining, and you-know-what. I explained to Joe my cat where I'd been all that time and why. He didn't seem to be very interested because, before my tale was done, he went to sleep on the galley bench.

Three days later, I sat in my usual booth at The Drunken Parrot and resumed editing *Stoney's Downfall* with the deadline breathing hard upon my neck. I picked up the story at the point where Stoney had been told by his snitch, Jake the Snake, that Father Ferguson had been killed by a leg-breaker sent by a bookie he was in debt to, and not by the prime suspect, Roland Jeffries:

The job now was to figure out which bookie owned Father Ferguson's gambling debts. In Chicago, that narrowed it down to a large portion of the underworld population.

Where to begin? With police arrest records of bookies who'd been caught and charged with illegally accepting bets, Stoney decided.

He sat in front of his desktop computer and logged into the departmental database. The search turned up too many names to deal with, so he narrowed it to only include people with multiple arrests within the previous three years who were not incarcerated. That produced a more manageable list. He decided to start with the top ten, based upon numbers of arrests.

Number one was a guy named Harry Del Monte. Like the ketchup, Stoney thought. Stoney was a Heinz man, not that it mattered, because if Harry was related to the Del Monte ketchup family, he wouldn't be taking sports bets in Chicago.

Harry's last known address was an upscale condo building on Michigan Avenue. His bookie business must be doing well, Stoney reflected. The record also reported that Del Monte owned a bar called The Four Aces on Wells Street. The name sounded familiar to Stoney. He'd been there a few years ago, when one customer stabbed another to death in a dispute over the last available barstool. The murder weapon was a Swiss Army knife. Short blade. Many stabs. The corkscrew came into play.

The Four Aces was a good place to start, Stoney decided. He drove there and parked his unmarked brown Taurus out front beside a fire hydrant. He went inside and breathed in the aroma of stale beer and cigarette smoke. If nothing else, he could bust Del Monte for violating the city's no-smoking law.

The Four Aces looked like any other sports bar in the city, its main feature being the many large-screen TVs which were tuned to various sporting events and were being watched by customers, aka illegal gambling clients, aka suckers.

Stoney took a seat at the bar. There were several open stools, which diminished the chance of a knife fight. The nearest TV was tuned to a soccer game. He considered soccer to be the second most boring of all sports, behind curling. Players ran around for what seemed an eternity, dribbling, passing, and heading the ball, until finally someone scored a goal, making the final tally one-zip. In a real barn burner, the ending score might be two-zip, or two-to-one. This game was taking place in England, Stoney could tell, because of the kinds of products being advertised, including Newcastle Brown Ale, which, he noticed, was available at The Four Aces on tap.

The bartender came over. Stoney ordered a Newcastle. When it arrived, he asked the bartender, a skinny young man with a nose ring, "Is the proprietor on the premises?"

The question was met with a blank stare. Stoney figured the guy didn't understand the two "p" words, so he rephrased the question: "Is Harry Del Monte here?"

"Yeah, he's in the back," the kid bartender said, then just stood there looking at Stoney.

This witness needs prompting, Stoney thought, so he said, *"If it's not too much trouble, can you get him for me?"*

The kid shrugged, which could have meant yes, or no. Finally, he came out from behind the bar and walked down a hallway to the back of the establishment. He returned a few minutes later, went back behind the bar, and began washing glasses without telling Stoney if Del Monte was available or not.

Just for the hell of it, Stoney asked him, *"What kind of ketchup do you serve here?"*

His answer was *"Huh?"*

Before Stoney could repeat the question, a man appeared from the back hallway, scanned the barroom, and walked over to Stoney. He looked like a man who needed to hire muscle to collect debts because he had none. Muscles, not debts. He was of less-than-medium height, in his fifties, bald, with a beer belly that jiggled when he walked, and the pasty white complexion of an indoor worker, which bookies are.

"Darrell says someone wants to see me," Del Monte said. *"That you?"*

"I'm the one," Stoney answered.

"About what?"

"Guy I know says I can find some action here."

"What guy and what kind of action?" Del Monte asked.

"A guy who wants to remain anonymous and the action being wagering on sporting events," Stoney answered.

"Anonymous doesn't cut it and betting is illegal," Del Monte said. *"So if that's all you got . . ."*

"I got one more thing," Stoney said, and flashed his gold shield.

I heard someone say my name and looked up from the manuscript. It was Alice Radinsky, my cook. She was holding a plate with something in a hamburger bun.

"I think I've finally got it," she said.

"Got what, Alice?"

"The recipe for those sloppy joe sandwiches you told me about, the ones they serve at that Sloppy Joe's Bar in Key West. I called there and the cook said he couldn't give me the recipe. No surprise.

I won't give out my recipe for creamed chipped beef on toast, beloved by battalions of gyrenes. So I've been experimenting."

She put the plate in front of me. "See what you think."

I picked up the sandwich, took a bite, and said, "No reason for me to ever go to Key West again."

24.

Lien on Me

Lucy Gates came through for me once again. I'd called and asked her to "drill down" into Stewart Leverton's business dealings. She reported that Leverton Properties was known for perpetually stiffing its subcontractors and for violating city construction codes, and that, over the last year or so, those nonpayments had gotten worse. I needed to find out if that was because the company had a money problem that prompted its owner to order Henry Wilberforce's murder so his wife could get an expected inheritance.

If it looks like a clue, smells like a clue, and walks like a clue, it's a clue. Or not.

Libby was not the kind of person to hire a hit man, it was clear by then. If it came to light, she would have been drummed out of The Mayflower Society. How very embarrassing. But she would know if Stewart was financially strapped and that their best source of funds for them was Uncle Henry's estate. I now didn't believe that Libby really kept her trip to see me secret from Stewart. More likely, they both decided she should tell me that because her accusation of Scooter would seem more credible if I thought she was having a crisis of conscience. They were in it together.

Sherlock Holmes told his sidekick Doctor Watson: "How often have I said to you when you have eliminated the impossible, whatever remains, however improbable, must be the truth."

Elementary.

In a real-life whodunit, half the job is figuring out whodunit. The other half is proving it.

I caught a flight from Fort Myers to Boston, which was beginning to feel like my second home. After Lucy's report on Stewart's problems with his subcontractors, I decided I'd start by interviewing them to try to gauge the magnitude of the financial bind he was in and see where that led.

We landed at Logan and I called Danny O'Rourke from the taxi. He said that my cubicle wasn't available because Detective Steve Bancroft had finally passed his kidney stone and was back on the job, but I could use O'Rourke's desk because he'd be out on a case for a while.

I went into the headquarters building and took the elevator up to the Homicide Unit. O'Rourke wasn't there, but Steve Bancroft was at his desk. I introduced myself and said, "I kept your chair warm for you."

He was a man of about fifty, wearing an expensive glen-plaid suit with a white button-down oxford-cloth shirt and a blue tie. He swiveled his chair around and said, "If you ever get a kidney stone, pal, shoot yourself."

"I'll keep that in mind," I told him.

"I was just going to get a cup of coffee," he said. "Join me?"

"Love to," I said.

We went to the coffee room. Bancroft knew how to work the espresso machine and asked if I wanted coffee or "one of those foo-foo drinks."

"When you put it that way, make it a coffee," I answered.

When he'd extricated two cups of coffee from the machine, he went to one of the cabinets, opened it, moved a stack of dishes, and came out with two glazed doughnuts. He winked at me and said, "Everyone has their own hidey-hole."

We went back to his cubicle. I pushed O'Rourke's chair over to where I could chat with Bancroft as we had our coffee and doughnuts.

"Danny told me about your case, Jack," Bancroft said. "Where does it stand?"

I explained where I was with Stewart and Libby Leverton.

"Danny's in the middle of a big investigation," he said. "Someone murdered a Catholic priest. But I'm in between cases, so I can go with you to talk to those subcontractors if you want."

Wow. The murder of a Catholic priest. Just like in Bill's new novel. Life imitates art.

"Sure, that'd be great," I told him. "If only to help me find them."

"Roger that," he said. "Getting around downtown can be a bit tricky."

I followed Bancroft outside to the parking lot and we got into his unmarked brown Taurus. First stop was a company called Shamrock Electric in Brookline.

Shamrock Electric was located in a single-story, tan-brick building on Boylston Street, just one street over from the ballpark. Bancroft parked on the street in front of the building in a legal space, no fire hydrant or loading zone being available. I'd called to make an appointment with the company's owner, a man named Tiny Berger. In my experience, a man named Tiny was anything but. Which proved to be the case when the receptionist told us Berger was in the shop, "Right through that door."

The shop was an open, expansive space consisting of rows of metal shelves holding various electrical components and an open area with benches where several women were seated, at work assembling electrical thingies.

A very large man wearing a plaid shirt, jeans, and cowboy boots was standing beside a bench, chatting with one of the women. We walked over and I said, "Mr. Berger? I'm Detective Starkey and this is Detective Steve Bancroft."

"Mr. Berger was my father," he said. "Call me Tiny."

"Works for me," Bancroft said.

"You said you wanted to talk about that sonofabitch Stewart Leverton," Tiny told me.

"I'm investigating a murder in Naples, Florida, and Leverton might have some information about it," I responded.

"Let's go to my office," Not-So-Tiny said, and we followed him to a room in a corner of the shop. It had unpainted Sheetrock walls with a window overlooking the shop floor. We all went inside. Tiny closed the door, sat behind his cluttered desk, and nodded us toward two side chairs. When Tiny dropped into his desk chair it made a groaning sound as if protesting the load.

When we were seated, Tiny said, "Leverton Properties hired us about two years ago to do all the electrical work for a big shopping mall development in Woburn. We did the job and still haven't been paid. He claims we did shoddy work and he had to hire another electrical contractor to redo everything. Which is complete bullcrap. He owes us north of a hundred grand. We slapped a mechanic's lien on the property, which doesn't get us paid, it only means we can ask the court for a judicial foreclosure sale and get our money from the proceeds. But that takes time. Years. That's what guys like Leverton count on. They either hold onto our money, interest free, until it's convenient for them to pay, or they negotiate a settlement for a lot less than what's owed."

Tiny opened a wooden humidor on his desk, extracted a cigar, used a silver cutting tool to snip off the tip and a butane lighter to fire it up, took a luxurious inhale, and asked if we'd like one of his stogies. "Cohibas," he said. "Got a pal who brings them to me from Toronto, Cuban cigars still being illegal in this country."

The Cohiba smelled great, but we both declined.

Tiny looked at Bancroft and said: "You're not going to arrest me for having these contraband cigars, are you?"

Bancroft smiled. "Got bigger fish to fry, Tiny."

"Why did you decide to work for a man like Stewart Leverton?" I asked him.

"Business was slow," he answered. "And I didn't know he *was* a man like that. It was our first job for him."

"I suppose your experience with him was not unique," Bancroft commented.

"I've since learned that the plumbing and HVAC subs also have liens on the same property. If you look into it, I'm sure you'll find that situation with Leverton's other developments."

Tiny took another puff on the cigar, held it up horizontally in front of his face, smiled, and said, "A woman is only a woman, but a good cigar is a smoke."

"You a fan of Rudyard Kipling?" I asked him. That was a line from his poem, "The Betrothed," a favorite of mine.

"Couldn't graduate from Cathedral High School without passing English Lit," he answered.

"Hey," Bancroft said, "I went there, too, but I must have missed that day."

I stood, followed by Bancroft, and said, "Thanks much for your time, Tiny."

"Not a problem," he said, adding, "Just curious. You mentioned a murder. Does Florida have the death penalty?"

"It does," I answered.

"Good," he said.

25.

The Enforcer

When we got back to the Taurus, Bancroft asked, "You got enough on Leverton for me to get a warrant to look at his financials?"

"Not yet."

He pulled away from the curb. "Where to next?"

I looked at notes I'd made on my legal pad and said, "The Carpenters Local Union 327 in Dorchester, 1252 Massachusetts Avenue." I looked at my watch. "We're running a little late."

"Not a problem," Bancroft said and turned on the Taurus's lights and siren.

"So what's this guy's name?" Bancroft asked as we rolled up to the Carpenters Union building and parked at the curb.

"It's a she," I said. "First name Rae, that's R-A-E. Last name, believe it or not, is Carpenter."

"Rae Carpenter, president of the Carpenters Union." Bancroft chuckled. "Like me being named Steve Detective."

We got out of the car and went into the grey single-story, wood-frame building. No concrete block construction for the carpenters. The front door chimed when we opened it and, after a moment, a woman appeared from a hallway. She was young, with short brown hair, late twenties I guessed, very attractive, and she was wearing a Suffolk Law School sweatshirt and khaki slacks.

"Can I help you?" she asked us.

"We're looking for Rae Carpenter," I told her. "She's expecting us. Detectives Jack Starkey and Steve Bancroft."

"That'd be me," she said. "Let's go to my office."

We followed her down the hallway and into an office. She gestured us to a leather sofa and rolled the desk chair out for herself. The office was a veritable man cave: stuffed game fish on the knotty-pine walls, a mounted deer head, various Boston sports memorabilia around the room, a silver hammer on a plaque, and a framed photo of a husky man in a plaid shirt and jeans standing near the home plate of a baseball field with another man in a Red Sox uniform whom I recognized as Carl Yastrzemski.

Rae smiled at what she knew was the incongruity of herself in this male environment.

"This was my dad's office until he died just under a year ago," she said. "Raymond Carpenter. My mom died when I was ten. I grew up on construction sites and joined the union when I was sixteen. I worked carpentry summers during college. I'm in my third year of law school. When dad died, the union officers asked me to fill in for him as interim president. I keep asking when they'll identify permanent candidates for the job, but so far they haven't done that."

"As I said when I called, I'm investigating a murder in Florida and you might have some information that would be helpful," I told her. "Detective Bancroft of the Boston Police Department is assisting me while I'm here."

"You mentioned Stewart Leverton when you called," she said.

"He's a person of interest," I told her. "What experience has your union had with his company?"

She frowned. "The worst. We won't work on Leverton Properties jobs anymore."

"Why is that?" Bancroft asked her.

"About a year ago, we had two guys hurt at one of their job sites. They weren't following proper safety procedures. When dad complained, they did nothing, so he threatened a strike. They sent a guy to talk to dad at the site. Bobby Amendola. He said he was vice president of security for Leverton Properties. Amendola said he hoped there wouldn't be any more accidents. It was a threat. A few days later, the union struck the site and put up picket lines. That night, my dad's house burned down. Dad was asleep. The smoke detectors went off and he got out. Dad knew Amendola had done it. But there was no proof."

"I remember that," Bancroft said.

"Then what happened?" I asked her.

"The strike continued for another two weeks. There were anonymous threats to union members. Calls in the middle of the night. One guy's truck was set on fire in his driveway."

"Our detective, Tom Laredo, looked into that but he couldn't tie those incidents to Leverton Properties," Bancroft said.

"How did it end?" I asked Rae.

"Dad died of a heart attack at his desk right here in this office," she said. "I know it was from the stress. I called the *Boston Globe* and they did a story. Then the Boston building department ordered Leverton Properties to correct the safety violations. They did. The union ended the strike, but we wouldn't go back to work there, so they finished with another contractor. We're in court with Leverton now over the money we're owed. About seventy thousand dollars."

"I'm sorry to hear about your dad, Rae," I said. "Thank you for your help."

As Bancroft and I were leaving her office, she asked, "Does Florida have the death penalty, Detective Starkey?"

"Yes, it does," I answered.

"Good," she said.

Back in the Taurus, Bancroft said, "Interesting that Stewart Leverton has an enforcer on his payroll. That Amendola guy."

"We've got two more union officials to see," I said. "But I'll postpone them so we can go back to headquarters and see what we can find out about Bobby Amendola."

On the way, I called Lucy Gates and asked her to see if she could find an electronic trail connecting Amendola to Stewart Leverton or Leverton Properties. She said she'd get back to me right away.

When I ended the call, Bancroft said, "I don't want to know about that, do I?"

"Know about what?" I answered.

"Right," he said.

At the office, Bancroft fired up his desktop computer, typed on the keyboard while I stood looking over his shoulder, and Bobby Amendola's police record came up on the screen.

"Okay, he's in the system," Bancroft said.

He used his mouse to scroll down the file.

"Let's see . . . Stole a car when he was thirteen, suspended sentence in juvie court . . . Aggravated assault at fifteen, sentenced to three months in the Worcester County Detention Center . . . Did adult time at eighteen in MCI-Framingham, two years for breaking and entering . . . Yada yada yada. Our boy's got a rap sheet as long as a Red Sox fan's hatred of the Yankees."

"Military service?"

He scrolled down and said, "When he was twenty-four, a judge gave him a choice. Enlist in the army or go to prison for assault."

"You got his military record in there?"

Bancroft scrolled and said, "Nope. But he must have been discharged early because, just over a year later, he was back in Boston losing his license for a DUI."

"I'm betting he doesn't have an honorable discharge certificate hanging on his wall at home," I said.

"There's more," Bancroft told me. "But you get the picture. He was a criminal and a thug from the get-go."

"Yet he ended up as vice president of security for Leverton Properties."

Bancroft hit a few keys and up came mug shots of Bobby Amendola through the years, looking meaner and tougher each time. In the most recent one, from three years ago, he was a forty-two-year-old man with cold dark eyes, a furrowed brow, a buzz cut, and the crooked nose of a fighter.

"Let me try something," I said.

I found the number for Leverton Properties under recent calls on my cell phone, hit the call button, and put the phone on speaker.

"Leverton Properties, how may I help you?" the receptionist answered.

"I'd like to speak with Bobby Amendola," I told her.

"I'm sorry," she said. "We have no one here by that name."

No surprise. I thanked her and ended the call.

"He's either gone, or employed off the books," I said. "Off the books is my guess."

"I wonder if he took the Leverton jet to Naples," Bancroft commented.

"What's his last known address?" I asked.

He logged on to the DMV website, entered a police password, waited for the secure site to come up, and said, "Here it is . . . 2409 Allenton Road in Billerica . . . Huh."

"What?"

"It's interesting that he chooses to live in a town with a county lockup. The Middlesex Jail and House of Correction. Must make him feel right at home."

"How far is Billerica from here?" I asked him.

"About a forty-five-minute drive." He smiled. "That's without lights and siren."

"Better to not let him know we're coming," I said.

We went outside to Bancroft's car and he programmed Amendola's address into Google Maps on his cell phone, saying, "I've been to Billerica to visit the detention facility. But I don't know the residential areas."

Traffic was heavy. Driving at the speed of civilians, we rolled up in front of a white two-story, wood-frame house which the Google Maps lady said was our destination. A concrete driveway led to a detached, two-car garage behind the house. A mailbox on a pole in front with the house number on it had its red flag up to alert the postman to outgoing mail. There was a black Cadillac Escalade parked in the driveway.

"Nice house, nice wheels," Bancroft commented. "The murder and intimidation business must pay well."

"Let's go ring the doorbell and fake it till we make it," I said.

Bancroft drove down the block, out of sight of the house, and parked in front of a fire hydrant. We got out of the Taurus and Bancroft said, "I've got two vests in the trunk. We are, after all, calling on a possible killer."

We went around to the trunk. He popped open the lid, pulled out two Kevlar vests, and handed one to me. Also in the trunk were two combat helmets, a twelve-gauge shotgun, an AR-15 assault rifle, a Heckler & Koch MP5 machine gun, boxes of shotgun and rifle shells, a cardboard box with hand grenades, probably flash-bangs, and a grey plastic-sided briefcase.

"Sweet Jesus, Steve," I said. "You got enough weaponry in there to arm an infantry platoon."

"Better than being left holding your dick in a gunfight," he said.

"What's in the briefcase?"

He grinned. "A little something for those long stakeouts. It's a bartender's kit with two shot glasses and a bottle of Maker's Mark."

I slipped off my leather jacket, put on one of the vests, adjusted the fit with the Velcro straps, and put my jacket over it. Bancroft opened the rear driver's side door, took off his suit coat, folded it and placed it on the seat, put on the other vest, took a tan raincoat from the seat, and slipped it on over his vest.

Like me, he was carrying a Glock in a belt holster at the small of his back. We both took out our pistols, checked to make certain that a shell was chambered, and put them back into the holsters.

I saw Bancroft smile and wave toward the single-story redbrick house we were parked in front of. I looked at it and saw an older woman peering out at us from between the curtains. She waved back and disappeared.

As we walked down the sidewalk to Amendola's house, Bancroft said, "I wonder if he lives alone."

"People in his line of work usually do," I said. "Unless they have a pit bull."

We went up the walk to Amendola's front door and I rang the bell. Bancroft, with his Glock in his hand, stood off to one side where he couldn't be seen by whomever answered the door.

No response. I rang the bell again. I heard footsteps on a wooden floor.

The door opened and a very large man, shirtless, with a scowl on his face, said, "What the fuck do you want?"

Amendola in the flesh.

Thinking on my feet, I said, "We were just wondering if Leverton Properties offers you a good benefits package."

Bancroft showed himself and added, "Health care, with dental?"

Amendola looked at us as if deciding whether or not to slam the door or to say, "Just a minute," and come back with a gun. Instead of either of those options, he said, "Never heard of Leverton Properties."

"A little bird told us you're in the company's employ, Bobby," I said.

I noticed that his right hand was out of sight behind the door jamb. I did a quick calculation. He wouldn't be holding a shotgun or rifle in one hand, too awkward, so it was a pistol. Even at close range, our Kevlar vests would stop a .44 Magnum or .45 ACP round, although we'd have very sore ribs for a long time. But 9mm and .357 bullets travel faster and could penetrate our vests.

While I was working that through, Amendola asked, "What little bird, and who the fuck are you guys?"

"We never reveal sources and methods," Bancroft told him. "As to our identity, we are your worst nightmare."

Rather dramatic but I liked it.

"Beat it, assholes," Amendola said, and slammed the door.

26.

Code Violation

We walked back to the Taurus, slipped off our vests, put them in the trunk, got in the car, and Bancroft said, "We got his attention. What next?"

"I want to try Libby Leverton again," I said, and gave him the address.

Bancroft pulled away from the curb and said, "We might need to armor up with the Kevlar again."

"Why's that?"

"That's a high-crime neighborhood."

"Beacon Hill is a high-crime neighborhood?"

"In the sense that you have to commit crimes to afford to live there."

Bancroft found the Levertons' row house without difficulty and we parked in front of my favorite fire hydrant. He waited in the car while I went to the door and rang the bell. I was getting good at it. The butler answered and I told him, "I need to speak with Mrs. Leverton about an important family matter."

He nodded and closed the door. When it reopened, Libby Leverton looked at me with a surprised expression and said, "I thought I made it clear that I have nothing more to say to you, Detective Starkey."

She was wearing a tennis outfit, no pearls. Wouldn't want to sweat on your Mikimotos while playing a match.

"There's been a new development," I told her. "We arrested Bobby Amendola on the charge of the murder of your Uncle Henry. Under interrogation, he implicated you and Stewart in the crime, in the sense that you ordered it."

Case law over the years had established that police can lie to suspects.

Libby drew in a breath and said, "It's cold out here. Come inside."

I followed her into the foyer and then into the living room, where a wood fire was burning in the fireplace. Very cozy. Maybe they planned Henry's murder sitting by that fireplace, swirling snifters of brandy. The decor was what I'd call Antique Robber Baron. Libby gestured toward a yellow sofa, where I sat, and she took an upholstered armchair beside me.

"I've never heard of that person, whatever his name is," she said.

"Bobby Amendola," I reminded her. "He is employed by your husband to do odd jobs and I think that your Uncle Henry was one of them."

She glared at me and said, "Now you must go away or we will sue you for harassment and whatever else our lawyer comes up with."

She could have told me that while I was standing on the front porch, but Mayflower Society members were too polite to leave a visitor out in the cold. It was now clear that Libby Leverton wasn't a pushover. A chain is only as strong as its weakest link and she was not one. After all, she'd gone to see me in Florida and, without flinching, pointed the finger of guilt at Scooter Lowry, and then faced me down here in Boston. I now had no doubt that she and Stewart were a murderous team who ordered the hit on Henry because they needed his inheritance money. But convincing myself and convincing the criminal justice system was a whole other ball game.

"Will there be anything else, Detective Starkey?" she asked.

"Are there any leftovers from your dinner party?" I asked her. "Maybe some lobster bisque, or a chicken leg to go?"

She looked at me like she didn't get my humor. Maybe I should have asked for scrod.

"Never mind. That covers it for now," I said, and followed her to the front door. She opened it and I went outside and back to the Taurus, got in, and told Bancroft, "Even under my withering interrogation, she didn't confess."

"A stand-up broad," he said, using a slang term for a female I hadn't heard since the days of Sinatra and his Rat Pack.

Lucy Gates called me as we were on the way to police head-quarters.

"If Bobby Amendola works for Stewart Leverton, they're careful about not leaving any evidence of it," she said.

"Okay, Lucy, thanks," I told her.

"Another call you didn't have?" Bancroft asked.

"Wrong number," I said.

We arrived at police headquarters, went inside and up to Homicide, where we found Danny O'Rourke in the coffee room.

"You guys solve Jack's case yet?" he asked us as he made a cup.

Bancroft held a thumb and index finger just a fraction apart and said, "We're this close to investigative glory."

"That last itty bit is always the hardest," O'Rourke said.

"How about your case?" I asked him as Bancroft made two cups of coffee for us. Obviously the Dunkin' Donuts box was a barren wasteland.

"That Catholic priest murder," O'Rourke said. "He was implicated in the sex-abuse scandal uncovered by the *Boston Globe* back in 2002, but he just got dead. Justice delayed. I busted my hump tracking down his victims and their families and friends, looking for suspects. I found six of the victims still living in the Boston area. Of those, only two agreed to talk to me. They both had alibis for the time of the murder. Their parents are deceased and the victims are certain that none of their other family members or friends would have killed the priest. Of the four who wouldn't talk, only one, on paper at least, seems capable of murder. He's in the system for various offenses, including assault. Nearly killed a guy in a bar fight. So I'm looking at him."

Bancroft and I walked over to his cubicle with our coffees. He sat at his desk and I rolled a chair over from an empty office.

"So how do we get Leverton to show his true colors?" Bancroft asked me.

"I think we need a decoy," I answered. Like all epiphanies, that had just occurred to me. "We find some way the decoy can really piss off Leverton, and then see if Amendola, ordered by Leverton, makes a run at him."

"Got anyone in mind to dangle in front of him?" Bancroft asked.

"That will follow from the plan," I said.

"Which is?"

And, just like that, the details of a plan came to me, as if Saint Michael the Archangel was whispering it into my ear.

"I'm thinking that we arrange for a fake city building inspector to show up at a Leverton Properties job site," I said. "The inspector trumps up a violation of some kind, threatens to shut down the job, and lets it be known that, if a payment is made, the problem will go away, and that the inspector hasn't mentioned the violation to anyone else. Yet."

"Leverton must be used to shakedowns like that," Bancroft said. "Wouldn't he just pay the bribe?"

"Yeah, but then our inspector will say he's changed his mind and the price is now double. Leverton will realize that this will be an endless shakedown and conclude that the inspector should disappear."

"I like it," Bancroft said. "It would be a nice twist if the inspector was a woman," he added. "Less threatening."

"You have someone in mind?"

Bancroft said, "We have a corporal who wants to be a sergeant. An assignment like this could give her a boost."

I looked at him and smiled. "She wouldn't happen to be Danny's niece, would she?"

27.

Undercover Officer Ryan

"I'm in," Millie said after I'd outlined the operation over lunch at the No Name Restaurant, a little seafood place on the Boston Fish Pier which, Millie told me, began in 1917 as a seafood stand serving fresh catches to commercial fishermen.

I decided to have our meeting over lunch so Millie could become accustomed to my investigative style. Her father was a swordboat captain, she said, and she'd been eating at the No Name since she was a young girl. In his honor, we both ordered grilled swordfish steaks, which were excellent. "Just out of the water," Millie said.

"You need to know that this assignment carries with it a high degree of risk," I told her. "The thug Stewart Leverton employs is as mean as they come. If I'm right, he's killed at least one person, and maybe more."

"Patrolling the streets of Boston carries with it a high degree of risk," Millie said. "So it'll be no different than a normal day at work."

"Okay," I said. "The head of the building department, a man named Bernie Shepard, is on board."

I gave her five business cards and a cell phone belonging to a real city building inspector named Judy Kykendall. Judy's supervisor told her that they were needed as part of a confidential investigation. She readily agreed when promised three days of paid leave.

We didn't want two Judy Kykendalls out there while working our scam.

The waitress appeared to ask about dessert.

"The bread pudding is a must," Millie said.

We both ordered some.

"Have you picked a job site?" she asked.

"Shepard told me that Leverton Properties is putting up a luxury hotel on Boston Harbor," I told her. "It's a big project that's just broken ground. The mayor was there to cut the ribbon. They won't want any problems with it."

"How much should I ask for?"

"If it's too small an amount it won't seem authentic," I said. "Too much, and they might make a run at you before we're ready. Ten thousand should be about right."

"When do I start?" Millie asked.

"First thing in the morning. I cruised the site. The foreman works out of a trailer. You'll find him, give him a business card, and tell him there's a problem with their soil sample. Shepard said that their soil sample's already been approved, but you'll say further analysis has raised a question about the groundwater, and they'll have to stop construction until it's resolved. The foreman will probably ask how long that will take, and you'll say things are really backed up, it could be six to eight weeks."

"That's when I'll tell him that maybe the problem can be made to disappear," Millie said.

"Exactly," I said. "I have no reason to think that the foreman is dishonest, but he'll likely be accustomed to shakedowns like this, so he'll take it to his boss, Stewart, and the rest should unfold as planned."

"And if it doesn't?"

"Let's stay positive," I told her.

"One more thing," Millie said. "What should I wear?"

Just like a woman, I thought, but, of course, didn't say, not in this #MeToo day and age.

"Jeans, boots, a flannel shirt if you have one, any kind of jacket," I said. "I've got a Boston building department hard hat for you in my car."

"Any makeup?" she asked. "Smoky eyes?"

I didn't have an answer for that one.

She laughed. "Just kidding, Jack."

The next morning, I was sitting in the Homicide Unit's conference room with Bancroft, waiting for Millie to report what happened at the hotel job site. Time passed slowly as we drank our coffee and split the one doughnut that was left.

After an hour, Millie showed up in her building inspector outfit with her hard hat tipped at a jaunty angle. She was wearing a tan canvas Carhartt jacket over her red plaid flannel shirt.

She gave a salute and said, "Undercover Officer Ryan reporting for duty."

"Tell us," Bancroft said, clearly pleased to see her alive and in one piece. As was I.

"The foreman's name is Randy Murphy," she said as she took a chair. "He seems like a straight shooter. And a hunk, I'll add. If he doesn't go to prison, we might have a future together. Or I could wait for him if it's not too long a sentence."

"How did he react?" I asked.

"I introduced myself, gave him the business card, and went through the script. He listened without showing any emotion, like it was routine business. As you predicted, he said he'll talk to headquarters and get back to me. I told him to call me on my cell phone, rather than at the building department, wink wink."

Randy Murphy, Leverton's foreman, called Millie the next morning and told her to meet him at the job site. I instructed her to have her gun with her, and if a big man, Bobby Amendola, was there, with or without the foreman, to make an excuse and leave immediately.

The three of us had lunch at Tony's, a nearby sub sandwich shop where cops got a discount, so we could rehearse the operation one more time. Then Bancroft and I went back to the office and Millie, driving a Ford F-150 truck Bancroft borrowed from the building department, drove to the hotel job site.

Millie returned to Homicide forty-five minutes later carrying a black canvas briefcase and said, "It was just Randy Murphy, the foreman, in the trailer. He told me that his boss agreed to the payment and handed me this briefcase, saying that it contained ten thousand dollars. I took it and told him that it was just a down payment and I needed ten thousand more. He said he'd check again with headquarters and call me with an answer."

"You don't have to go any farther with this," I told Millie. I was having second thoughts about her safety. "We can always find another way."

"That other way being?"

I was silent, and she said, "That's what I thought."

Millie, Bancroft, and I hung around the office, chatting about life on the job, fishing, and hunting.

Judy Kykendall's cell phone rang.

"Hello?" Millie said into the phone.

She listened, saying "Uh huh" several times, "All right," and finally, "That works for me," and ended the call.

"Murphy said the second payment has been approved," she told us, "and that I should meet him at nine tonight at the Charlestown Navy Yard."

"No surprise," Bancroft said. "It's part of a big park. A secluded location at night, when everything there will be closed. And, of course, it will be Amendola who shows up, not Murphy."

"What's there?" I asked Millie.

"Two ships, *Old Ironsides* and a World War II destroyer, the *USS Cassin Young*, that also serves as a museum ship. Other than that, there's a museum and a visitor center. Murphy told me to meet him in the parking lot of the visitor center."

"You know your local history," I said.

"All of Boston is local history," she told me. "School kids learn it all by heart."

"We need to get Lieutenant Halloran to sign off," Bancroft told us.

"We'll do that, but let's start with a tour of the Charlestown Navy Yard," I said.

I rode shotgun in the Taurus, with Millie in the back seat, as Bancroft navigated our way to Charlestown. Along the way, Millie continued her tour-guide narration: "The Charlestown Navy Yard was originally known as the Boston Navy Yard, established in 1800 as a navy shipbuilding facility. It was in continuous service until it was decommissioned in 1974. The property is now part of the thirty-acre Boston National Historical Park."

"Now here's a truly historic site," Bancroft said as he pulled over and parked at the curb in a loading zone. "Louie's Lunch Bucket, my favorite burger joint. Bacon double cheeseburgers to die for."

He flinched, realizing that saying "to die for" was not a good thing under the circumstances, the circumstance being that Millie was soon to be a decoy for a probable killer.

She broke the tension by starting to laugh and saying, "No better place for a last meal than Louie's."

Bancroft was right about the burgers. Maybe, because she was nervous, Millie ate like it was her last meal. Bancroft and I matched her, just to put her at ease.

It was a fifteen-minute drive from Louie's to the Fifth Street entrance of the Charlestown Navy Yard. We drove down a winding road, past buildings that certainly looked historic, but I refrained from asking Millie, the local history buff and show-off, about them. We pulled into a parking lot filled with cars and school buses. A sign said that the lot was for the visitor center, which was a one-story redbrick building.

We got out of the Taurus and walked to the front of the visitor center building. From there, I could see piers running into Boston Harbor with the *USS Constitution* and the destroyer Millie mentioned moored to one of them.

"The *Constitution*, aka *Old Ironsides*, was launched in 1798 and is the oldest commissioned ship in the navy," Millie told me as we looked at the piers. "She never lost a battle. I can tell you about each one . . ."

"I don't doubt that for a second," I said.

Bancroft laughed and said, "Maybe another time, Millie. We've got work to do."

We walked the area, then got back into the Taurus and drove around the park, noting the buildings, how the roads came together, and the entrance-exit streets. On the way back to police headquarters, Bancroft said, "Given the layout, here's what I recommend. At eight P.M., Jack and I will drive back there and park behind the Constitution Museum building, out of sight. Millie will arrive at eight thirty in the department's armored vehicle."

"Tell me about that," I said.

"It's an unmarked Ford Utility SUV with the Police Interceptor package that's up-armored like a Humvee in a war zone," he told me. "It would take an armor-piercing bullet to go through the metal or the glass."

"Go on," I told him.

"Millie parks in the visitor center lot as instructed," he continued. "Amendola will arrive at nine, he said, and Millie will stay in the Ford with the doors locked and windows up. When she doesn't get out, Amendola will walk over, carrying an empty briefcase. He'll tell her to get out. Instead, she'll point her pistol at him. He'll assume she can shoot him through the glass so he'll shoot first, at the glass, and then probably at the door. When his bullets don't pierce either one, and given that he's not killed by the ricochets, he'll know he's been had and run back to his car. We'll block the road, with Millie driving up behind him. If he tries to drive over the park grounds, I'll have a police helicopter on call to follow him and squads ready to block him."

"If we take Amendola alive we can charge him with attempted murder of a police officer, even though he doesn't know Millie is one," I said. "Then I can see if his gun matches the weapon used in the Naples killing. We recovered the bullet."

"And if it does, we offer him a plea bargain in return for cooperating in the prosecution of the Levertons," Millie said.

"Now we need to brief Lieutenant Halloran," Bancroft said.

Back at headquarters, the three of us found Lieutenant Halloran in his office. I let Bancroft explain the details of our operation. Halloran listened, stroked his chin, and said, "Are you okay with this, Corporal Ryan? It's purely a volunteer assignment."

Millie nodded and said, "I am, sir."

Halloran turned to me and said, "You get one of our officers killed, Starkey, and the Naples PD won't recognize you when we give you back."

"Roger that," I said.

28.

Baiting the Trap

We had several hours to kill before it was time to set up the trap at the Charlestown Navy Yard for Bobby Amendola, so we went back to the office, where Bancroft attended to his other cases, Millie went to the squad room, and I sat in Danny O'Rourke's empty cubicle and made calls to Tom Sullivan, my bartender Sam Longtree, and to Marisa. There was universal agreement that my latest plan might work, or it might fail spectacularly.

At seven thirty, Bancroft and I took the elevator down a floor to the squad room to tell Millie it was time for him and me to depart for the Charlestown Navy Yard, ahead of her.

"Last chance to go to law school," I told her.

"The legal profession would seem mega-boring compared to this," she said.

Bancroft drove us to the Charlestown Navy Yard and parked in the rear lot of the Constitution Museum. While waiting, we chatted about sports, politics, and his retirement dream, which involved a lake cabin in Vermont with good bass fishing and satellite TV for all the sports channels.

Bancroft looked at his watch and said, "I've got Kevlar vests in the trunk."

We got out and put them on. At eight thirty, we heard a car drive by on the street in front of the museum: Millie in the armored

Ford SUV. A moment later, she called Bancroft on his cell phone to say she was in place.

A half-hour later, right at nine, we heard a car on the road. We got out of the Taurus, found we didn't have a clear line of sight to the visitor center parking lot, went back to the Taurus. Bancroft drove out onto the road, headlights off, and parked, far enough back to not be seen from the visitor center parking lot, but close enough, with the windows down, for us to hear gunshots.

A few moments later, we heard three of them.

Bancroft hit the gas and headed toward the visitor center just as we saw a pair of headlights coming at us. He skidded to a stop parallel to the road, a blocking move, and put the headlights on, along with the car's lights and siren. We got out and stood behind the open car doors. I had my Glock pointed at the oncoming car and Bancroft had the shotgun.

The game of chicken ended when Amendola was maybe twenty yards away. He swerved onto the grass of the park. He was driving his Escalade, which would have no trouble off-road.

Bancroft and I hopped back into the Taurus and he gunned it in pursuit of Amendola, lights and siren still on. He picked up his police radio microphone and said, "Dispatch, this is Detective Bancroft, badge number 1430, in pursuit of a black Cadillac Escalade, license number unknown. Subject is driving off-road at high speed through the Charlestown Navy Yard, passing the commandant's house and heading northwest toward the Thirteenth Street exit onto Chelsea Street."

"Roger that, Detective," came a woman's voice in reply. "What do you need?"

"Require units to block off Chelsea one mile east and west of Thirteenth and surveillance by Air One," Bancroft told her.

"We're on it," the dispatcher said. "Stay in touch and good hunting."

All the while, we were bumping over the ground at speed, gaining on the Escalade as it sped toward the park exit where we came in.

"If he goes out that exit," Bancroft said, "his only choices are to turn east or west, where he'll be blocked by our units, or to turn back into the park on Sixteenth Street going east, or on Fifth Street, going west."

I'd been in many high-speed pursuits, but none of them in a park. I heard the unmistakable whirring of helicopter blades through the open car windows.

"We've got him now," Bancroft said.

His breathing was rapid, as was mine, and his hands gripped the wheel so hard his knuckles were white. The Escalade was fast, but no match for the Taurus's Police Interceptor engine. We came up on its rear bumper just as the police chopper came overhead and lit up the scene with a blinding spotlight. An amplified voice from the chopper said, "Police, halt! Police, halt!"

Which reminded me of a cop TV show I liked, *Blue Bloods*. However, something about that show always annoyed me. Whenever Danny or Jamie was approaching a suspect, he shouted out, from a distance: "Police! Stop! Police!" Of course, the suspect bolted. What you really did was sneak up on the bad guy until you were right on him and he couldn't escape. Another annoyance about *Blue Bloods* was that Danny, a detective played by Donnie Wahlberg, was always able to run the suspect to ground. Donnie was no spring chicken, but he could catch guys much younger as they sprinted through traffic, down alleys, and climbed over fences. Will Estes, who played Jamie, a uniformed officer, was a spring chicken, but he wore a heavy utility belt and black leather dress shoes, while the miscreant was usually wearing a track suit and Nikes, or some such outfit. Still, Jamie caught up with the guy. The show should hire me as a consultant. Then I'd have two incomes from the world of crime fiction.

Shouting out an order to halt was much more effective when it came from a helicopter hovering overhead.

Bancroft accelerated up close to the Escalade and, using a technique cops learn in driving school, turned the Taurus's right bumper hard into the left rear of the Escalade, causing it to fishtail and hit a massive oak tree head-on at high speed.

Bancroft skidded to a stop beside the Escalade and we hopped out, guns up. Right then, Millie's armored SUV arrived. It was safe, but too heavy to be fast. She got out with her pistol drawn. Bancroft extended his hand, palm out, toward her, telling her to stay back. He and I approached the Escalade, Bancroft on the driver's side and me on the passenger's side. Through the window, I could see that Amendola wasn't moving, with the air bag inflated against his chest and face.

"Like clockwork," Millie told us as she approached the Escalade. "He did exactly what you said he would. I think one of his bullets ricocheted off my window and caught him somewhere in his upper body. Never saw anyone look so friggin' surprised."

She was grinning.

The thrill of the hunt.

29.

Adrenaline Rush

The next time I saw Bobby Amendola, he was unconscious in a bed in a private room at Massachusetts General Hospital, his left wrist handcuffed to the bed frame and two uniformed Boston PD officers standing guard in the hallway.

It was nine the morning after the Charlestown Navy Yard adventure. A doctor, a young Asian woman, met us at the reception desk on the floor and told us that Amendola had suffered a concussion, broken ribs, a broken nose, and a deflated left lung. The name tag on her white coat said she was Dr. Linn.

"He has a chest wound from a gunshot, but most of the damage was done by the air bag," she told us. "He'll live."

"How long before we can haul his sorry ass to the Suffolk county jail?" Bancroft asked her.

"In two or three days," Dr. Linn said. "Now you'll have to excuse me while I attend to patients who aren't under arrest."

There was nothing more to do until we could sweat Amendola. Bancroft had other police business, so I hung around my hotel, working out in the exercise room, watching movies on TV, strolling around the city a few more times, and editing the Jack Stoney book.

On the second morning, having formed a bond with the Google Maps lady, I decided to go back to the Charlestown Navy

Yard to take a tour of *Old Ironsides* and the destroyer *USS Cassin Young*. Jack Starkey, the irrepressible tourist. My visit was considerably more enjoyable than my last time there. The two proud ships of the line, whose glory days were a century-and-a-half apart, were fascinating to see up close. They'd seen a lot more action than I ever would.

Tour guides described their histories. The *Constitution* was named by George Washington himself and her nickname, *Old Ironsides*, was given after a battle in 1812, with a British frigate off the Massachusetts coast. The two ships fired broadsides into each other, but the British cannonballs bounced off the *Constitution's* rugged oak sides, just like Amendola's bullets bounced off Millie's SUV.

On the third day, Bancroft and I visited Amendola again. He was in the hospital wing of the Suffolk County House of Correction. The day before, Bancroft had obtained and executed a search warrant for Amendola's Escalade, house, and electronic devices. Bancroft found no communications between Amendola and Leverton and Lucy Gates hadn't found anything incriminating by hacking into Stewart Leverton's devices. I didn't expect that she would. They'd do business face-to-face. Also nothing helpful to our case in his home. But we did recover his .22-caliber Ruger semiautomatic pistol from the smashed-up Escalade after the chase in the park.

The slugs he fired into Millie's SUV were too badly damaged to make a match with his Ruger, but we didn't need one to charge him with the attempted murder of a police officer. We had a very nice video of the whole thing from the camera in Millie's vehicle. And the Boston PD crime lab did match the Ruger to the bullet I brought with me from Henry Wilberforce's house.

Long story short, Amendola's ass was in a sling.

We found Amendola sitting in a wheelchair in the hospital wing's visitors' room. A guard had unlocked the door for us. The windows had wire mesh screens on them.

Seated in a folding chair beside Amendola was a young man wearing a suit. Amendola had deep yellow and purple bruises on his face and a metal splint on his nose. The young man stood up as we approached and said, "Detectives, I'm Rob Little, Mr. Amendola's attorney. I work for the Public Defender Division."

Just as I suspected, Stewart Leverton had not hired a lawyer for his enforcer. That would have established a connection between them. Without evidence of Amendola's employment, we had to get him to give up his boss.

Rob Little looked to be in his mid-twenties, a recent law school grad no doubt, with wire-rimmed glasses that gave him a studious look. It was clear from the cut of his suit that public defenders made minimum wage.

Bancroft and I found two folding chairs at a nearby table, pulled them over, and sat near Amendola and Little. I said, "We have a few questions for your client, counselor."

"That's fine," Little said. "And you do understand that he doesn't have to answer them."

"When he hears what we have to say, I think he'll want to," Bancroft said.

"We'll see," Little said.

"How are you feeling, Bobby?" I asked him.

"How the fuck do you think I'm feeling?" he said. "Just look at me."

"You shouldn't speed in the park," Bancroft told him. "It's dangerous, and against the law."

I looked at Little and said, "Your client has been charged with the attempted murder of a police officer. We've got it on videotape. We're also prepared to charge him with the murder of Henry Wilberforce in Naples, Florida."

"Never heard of him," Amendola said.

Little put his hand on Amendola's arm, indicating that he shouldn't talk about that. I didn't know if Amendola had told Little about Henry's murder. Probably not.

"Maybe you haven't heard of him, but your Ruger has," I said.

"I'll need to see the ballistic evidence of that," Little told me.

"Of course," I said. "But before we get into that we have a proposition."

"Which is?" Little asked.

"If Amendola will cooperate with us, we'll ask the Naples district attorney to consider taking the death penalty off the table and the Boston DA to consider a lesser charge for the attempted murder of a police officer."

"Define cooperation," Little said.

Little might be a recent law school grad working as a public defender, but he clearly knew his stuff. Clothes don't make the man.

"We know that Amendola was ordered to commit both of those crimes by his employer, Stewart Leverton," I said. "If he will testify to that, he has a chance of getting out of prison while he's still breathing."

Little looked at Amendola, then said to me, "I need to confer with Mr. Amendola privately."

"Sure," I said, and Bancroft and I found another guard to unlock the door to the hallway, and we left the room.

"Do you think Amendola will take the deal?" Bancroft asked me.

"Mentioning the death penalty usually does the trick," I said.

"Will your DA approve it?"

"Tom Sullivan, the Naples police chief, has already talked about it to her. She said that, once she reviews all the facts, she'll consider it. How about your DA?"

"That's Randall Wilcox. He's a hard ass. He'll want to nail Stewart Leverton if the evidence supports it."

A few minutes later, Little had the guard open the door and nodded at us to come back in. He said, "We'll need that proffer in writing, Detectives."

Bancroft and I left the prison and drove back to police headquarters. On our way to the coffee room in the Homicide Unit,

Rob Little called me on my cell phone and said, "Mr. Amendola is willing to testify in the way you described. Once we have the signed proffers from the two district attorneys, they can take his deposition and we can go from there."

"I'll get back to you as soon as we have them," I told him.

"In the meantime," Little said, "I want Mr. Amendola returned to Mass General, where he can get the proper treatment and rehab."

"I'll think about that," I said. After a moment, I said, "I thought about it and the answer is no." I was generally not in favor of mollycoddling skells like Bobby Amendola.

I ended the call and said to Bancroft, "Amendola's taking the deal. I'll have Tom Sullivan get the proffer document from our DA and you can do the same with yours."

Bancroft, the bass fisherman, said, "Fish on. Now let's reel him in, mount him, and hang him on the wall."

That night, Bancroft, Millie, and I met at Paddy O'Doul's Pub. The place was crowded with people celebrating whatever, maybe just the fact that it was Wednesday. During my drinking days, I celebrated Wednesday, too, as well as Sunday, Monday, Tuesday, Thursday, Friday, and Saturday. I'd told Bancroft that maybe we should wait to declare victory until we had Stewart Leverton behind bars, but he said, just in case that didn't happen, we wouldn't want to miss a good time at Paddy's. I couldn't argue with that logic.

"Halloran said he won't forget what you did," Bancroft told Millie after we ordered our drinks from the young waitress, who was wearing a white blouse, tartan skirt, and matching bonnet. Faith and begorra!

"I enjoyed the rush," she said.

"That means you're hooked on the job," I told her. "It doesn't happen all the time, there's a lot of frustration too. But there's enough to keep you going."

"In my case, for nineteen years and counting," Bancroft said.

30.

The Opera Singer

Two days later, Bobby Amendola had recovered enough to be taken in a police van to the offices of the Suffolk County district attorney for his deposition about the attempted murder of Corporal Millie Ryan. According to Massachusetts law, it didn't matter that Amendola thought Millie was a civilian when he fired three shots at her as she sat in her armored SUV which, of course, was also a crime. But shooting at a police officer was worse.

Bancroft and I weren't allowed to attend the deposition proceeding, which was conducted by an assistant district attorney. Amendola's lawyer, Rob Little, was present.

When the deposition was finished, the ADA, an experienced prosecutor named Ellie Gorman, called Lieutenant Halloran to report the results and Halloran passed the transcript on to Bancroft and me. Amendola had sung like Pavarotti at La Scala, in return for a recommended sentence of fifteen-to-twenty years, with the possibility of parole, in a Massachusetts state prison.

It was part of the agreement with Rob Little that, when Ellie Gorman finished her questioning, an assistant DA from Collier County, Florida, named Peter Boylan, who'd flown in for the occasion, got his turn with Amendola. Amendola's concert continued for Boylan.

The Suffolk County DA had enough incriminating evidence against Stewart Leverton, based on Amendola's testimony, to charge him with conspiracy to commit murder in Massachusetts, and the Collier County DA had enough to charge him with conspiracy to commit the murder of Henry Wilberforce in Naples. It was part of Amendola's plea bargain that he'd serve his time in Massachusetts, and then, if he survived, he'd stand trial in Collier County for murder, with a maximum sentence of life without parole.

Halloran reported that both ADAs said that Little provided Amendola with competent representation. That was important, not only to his client, but also to the prosecutors, because inadequate representation was grounds for appeal.

The day after the depositions, Randall Wilcox, the Suffolk County DA, placed a call to Stewart Leverton's attorney, Gilbert Norquist, to tell him that his client was being charged with conspiracy to murder a police officer and also about the pending Naples charge. Norquist was able to persuade Wilcox to allow Leverton to surrender to Detective Bancroft at police headquarters rather than having Bancroft arrest him at his home or office and perp-walk him to the detective's Taurus. Leverton was a pillar of the community, Norquist had argued, had never been in trouble before, and was not a flight risk.

Bancroft and I were told that the DA responded to those assertions by saying, "You mean we've never caught your client breaking the law before, counselor. If he hops a flight to Tahiti, I'll hold you responsible."

That night, Bancroft and I celebrated again at Paddy O'Doul's. Millie had a date with a fireman her Uncle Danny didn't approve of because he was a fireman and not a cop. Stewart Leverton was scheduled to surrender the next morning.

"Want to be there?" Bancroft asked me.

"My work here is done," I said. "Time to head for home until I have to come back for Leverton's trial."

No trial for Bobby Amendola, with his plea bargain in place. I'd have to appear at Leverton's trial as a witness to the attempted murder of Millie by Amendola. Bancroft, Millie, and the crew of the police helicopter were also on the witness list. Amendola would be the star witness.

Bancroft called the next day, while I was at my bar, and said, "Stewart Leverton didn't fly to Tahiti after all. He walked into police headquarters with his lawyer at seven this morning. I arrested him and he was arraigned for attempted murder before a district court judge, released on two million dollars bail, ordered to wear a monitoring ankle bracelet, and placed under house arrest until he appears in two weeks before the same judge to set a trial date."

"Keep me informed," I said.

Bancroft called me again two days later and reported that, during questioning at police headquarters, Stewart Leverton categorically denied that his wife, Libby, had any knowledge of the alleged crimes. Libby said the same thing when Bancroft questioned her.

"I tend to believe her, Jack," he said. "Even if I didn't, we have no evidence that she did know anything about the crimes, and she wouldn't be called to testify against Stewart because of the rule of spousal privilege."

"One out of two for the Levertons isn't a bad batting average," I said. "That's better than Ted Williams."

"What's next for you, Jack?" he asked.

"I'll be taking care of business. Non-police business."

He chuckled and said, "Come back to Boston any time you want to get scrod."

31.

Witnesses for the Prosecution

Two months later, I was back in Boston for Stewart Leverton's trial in Suffolk County District Court before Judge Anthony Merino and a jury of twelve men and women who, unless they were felonious, multimillionaire real estate developers, were definitely not the defendant's peers.

The three-day trial was big news in Boston. The courtroom gallery was packed with journalists and interested citizens, including Rae Carpenter, president of Carpenters Local Union 327, and other people Leverton had screwed and intimidated over the years. Libby Leverton was not there.

Gilbert Norquist, Stewart Leverton's personal lawyer, was not a criminal defense attorney, so Leverton hired Samuel Stein from New York, who was known as one of the best in the country.

And he was. His strategy was to go relatively easy on me, Steve Bancroft, Millie Ryan, and the two-man crew of the Boston PD helicopter. We all were law enforcement officers whom the jury was likely to find credible. Suffolk County ADA Jennifer Parsons questioned us. We gave practiced, straightforward answers about our investigation. Stein objected now and then, but he basically let us tell our stories.

After all, as Stein pointed out in his opening statement to the jury, our evidence was largely circumstantial. Nothing we would say would tie his client directly to the attempted murder of Corporal Millie Ryan by Bobby Amendola, Stein told the jury, and he was right. The only direct evidence that Leverton was guilty of conspiracy to commit murder would be the testimony of Bobby Amendola, Stein said, a career criminal who'd pleaded guilty to the underlying crime as part of a plea bargain in return for a reduced prison sentence.

As all good defense attorneys do, Stein offered an alternate theory of the case. He said that Bobby Amendola attempted to kill Millie "for reasons of his own, which he has refused to divulge in order to obtain a plea bargain from the district attorney by implicating my client."

Amendola had been brought to the Suffolk County Superior Courthouse at Three Pemberton Square from the Suffolk County House of Correction the morning of the first day of the trial. Both days he'd changed in a holding cell adjacent to the courtroom from his orange prison jumpsuit into a grey suit, white shirt, and blue tie provided by the DA's office. The DA forgot about shoes, so Amendola wore prison sneakers without laces. The US Supreme Court had ruled that prisoners appearing in court before a jury can wear civilian clothes, the theory being that if a defendant walked into the courtroom wearing black-and-white-striped PJs and dragging a ball and chain, he would be, in the eyes of the jury, already guilty.

First, ADA Parsons questioned her star witness about Amendola's employment by Leverton, including how Leverton had used Amendola as an enforcer for his various construction projects, and about the fake bribery by Millie, posing as a city building inspector at the Boston Harbor hotel project. Stein offered no objections during this questioning.

What happened next showed why the best criminal defense attorneys get paid the big bucks. When Parsons finished, Stein slowly rose from his seat beside Leverton and approached Amendola on the witness stand. A lion stalking a gazelle.

Here is an excerpt of Stein's cross examination from the trial transcript:

MR. STEIN: Now, Mr. Amendola, is it true that you've spent about half of your adult life in prison for various crimes?

MS. PARSONS: Objection, Your Honor. Prejudicial.

JUDGE MERINO: Mr. Stein?

MR. STEIN: Goes to the credibility of the witness.

JUDGE MERINO: Overruled. Mr. Amendola, you will answer the question.

MR. AMENDOLA: Yeah, that sounds about right.

MR. STEIN: In order to induce your testimony here today, is it correct that the district attorney has promised you a reduced sentence for the crime of attempted murder of a police officer, a crime you have pleaded guilty to?

(Mr. Amendola nods his head in the affirmative.)

MR. STEIN: Let the record show that the witness is acknowledging by the nodding of his head that he has been granted a reduced sentence in return for his testimony.

JUDGE MERINO: So noted.

MR. STEIN: Now, Mr. Amendola, will you explain to the jury why, given these circumstances, they should believe your testimony that you were employed by Mr. Leverton.

MR. AMENDOLA: Because I have an honest face?

(There is laughter from the stands.)

JUDGE MERINO (pounding his gavel): One more outburst like that from the stands and I will clear the courtroom.

MS. PARSONS: I object to that question, Your Honor. Mr. Amendola cannot possibly know what effect his testimony will have on the jury.

MR. STEIN: Until they render a verdict, that is.

MS. PARSONS: Objection . . .

MR. STEIN: I'll withdraw the question. Under questioning by Ms. Parsons, you alleged that Mr. Leverton had you on his payroll, correct?

MR. AMENDOLA: Correct.

MR. STEIN: So I assume you have proof of that employment? Payroll check stubs, bank deposits, income tax forms?

MR. AMENDOLA: I was always paid in cash.

MR. STEIN: How convenient.

MS. PARSONS: Objection. Counsel is testifying.

JUDGE MERINO: Sustained. Let's keep it to questions, Mr. Stein.

MR. STEIN: Was this alleged cash arrangement at your request or Mr. Leverton's?

MS. PARSONS: Objection. Mr. Amendola stated in his deposition to the district attorney that the cash payments were Mr. Leverton's idea.

MR. STEIN: My turn to object, Your Honor. What Mr. Amendola may or may not have said in that deposition was part of a plea arrangement with the district attorney related to the charge of attempted murder against Mr. Amendola and is not relevant to this proceeding.

JUDGE MERINO: Sustained.

It went on like that, and when Stein was done, Bobby Amendola came off as what he was: a career criminal who'd been paid off by the DA, and thus his testimony could reasonably be considered suspect.

The jury deliberated for only two hours at the end of the third day of the trial and returned a verdict of not guilty on the charge of conspiracy to commit murder. Which meant that, if Bobby Amendola was ever brought to trial in Collier County for the murder of Henry Wilberforce, there was little or no chance that a jury there would believe him about his relationship with Stewart Leverton any more than the Suffolk County jury did.

Leverton had gotten away with murder. He and Libby were free to continue their life of privilege.

Sometimes you eat the bear and sometimes the bear eats you.

32.

Any Crime Will Do

Marisa and I were having dinner at Lulu's Fish House on Estero Bay. We were seated at a table on the patio. The moon was full, the sky cloudless, the stars twinkling as if all was right with the world, which it wasn't, and rarely is. But you play the hand you're dealt and the best that you can hope for, so goes the Kenny Rogers song "The Gambler," is to die in your sleep.

"At least you got paid for your time, Jack," Marisa said after I'd gone over the hand I'd been dealt on my Naples homicide investigation.

"Which I feel guilty about," I said.

"Lawyers get paid whether their client wins or not."

"Which is why no one likes them."

"So Stewart Leverton gets off scot-free," she sighed, and sipped her wine.

"Actually, there's been an interesting development involving Stewart Leverton," I said. "Steve Bancroft, that Boston detective, called me yesterday. The Suffolk County district attorney has charged Leverton with crimes related to the bribery of city officials. His construction foreman, Randy Murphy, was arrested for his role in the bribery and offered a plea bargain in return for his testimony against Leverton. An investigation produced many witnesses about other such activities, going back many years. Amendola's testimony was not needed for that. So maybe Leverton will do a stretch in the pen after all."

"Like OJ," she said. "He gets off on one crime and they get him for another."

"Any crime will do," I said, and we raised our glasses in a toast to that, Marisa's filled with a nice pinot grigio and mine with an excellent diet root beer.

That night, lying in bed aboard *Phoenix*, I made a mental inventory of all that had happened following my lunch with Cubby Cullen when he told me about the murder of Henry Wilberforce and asked if I would meet with Naples Police Chief Tom Sullivan. The title of the Grateful Dead's second album was, "What a Long Strange Trip It's Been." Just like my investigation.

Scooter Lowry was happily living the life of a trust-fund slacker in Santa Monica. Good for him.

Bobby Amendola, who'd murdered Henry Wilberforce, was serving time for the attempted murder of a Boston police officer and, if he survived his sentence, would stand trial in Naples for the murder of Henry Wilberforce.

Stewart Leverton, who'd ordered that murder, but escaped prosecution because of the Boston result, was under indictment for the bribery of numerous Boston city officials, and his construction foreman, Randy Murphy, charged with the same crimes, was going to testify against him. There were consultants that people could hire to provide advice on how to deal with incarceration. One piece of advice presumably was to avoid dropping the soap in the shower.

Libby Leverton was still living the high life in her Beacon Hill row house, but she could be out on the street if Stewart's legal fees ate up the family fortune. She'd have to pawn her pearls, poor dear.

Lucy Gates called to tell me that she'd put an alert in her system to notify her of any news about my suspects. She found out that Alan Dumont had been killed, along with his wife, June, by the Larry Infante crime family of Providence, which had also murdered Daniel Danko, the Dirigo vice president of government relations, and Sheldon Sharkey, Dirigo's Washington lobbyist. The FBI had opened an investigation of Infante for the alleged bribery of federal government officials relating to the Dirigo's navy shipbuilding contract. Turned out that Dirigo's in-house counsel also knew about that and was going to testify to it. I called my friend Sarah Caldwell, a special agent in the bureau's Tampa Field Office, who helped me on a previous case. She told me that the bureau hoped that one or more of the crime family's soldiers would agree to give up their boss for more serious crimes. In return for a reduced sentence, maybe Larry Infante would reveal the location of Jimmy Hoffa's remains.

I had gained a level of confidence, if not total, for navigating the streets of Boston. I now knew what to order at Fat Thomas's Tavern.

Boston Detective Steve Bancroft was now attending AA meetings. He thanked me for the suggestion.

Millie Ryan had been promoted from corporal to sergeant with the Boston PD.

Her uncle, Detective Danny O'Rourke, had caught the killer of the Boston pedophile priest. It was the father of one of the victims. Which reminded me of Jack Stoney's case.

Rob Little, Bobby Amendola's public defender, had joined a prominent Boston law firm as an associate. He needed to pay off student loans. I hoped Rob would never become Shakespearean in his pursuit of billable hours.

Judy Kykendall, the Boston city building inspector whose identity Millie borrowed, was arrested and charged with accepting bribes from various real estate developers. Maybe I gave her the idea.

Rae Carpenter, interim president of Carpenters Local Union 327 in Dorchester, graduated from law school and accepted the union job permanently.

Lucy Gates, my computer hacker, called again and told me she was shutting down her business in Key West and moving to an unspecified location to do a confidential job. My guess: The federal government had enlisted her in the war against international cybercrimes. The nation would be safer for it.

Even though no one had yet been convicted of the murder I was hired to investigate, I cashed the City of Naples check for my consulting fee and made a donation in that amount to Collier County Habitat for Humanity in the names of Henry and Miriam Wilberforce. As Henry knew better than I did, philanthropy was good for the soul.

And then, Joe's rhythmic breathing at the foot of my bed and the lapping of waves against the double pontoon hulls of *Phoenix* lulled me into a deep sleep. REM might have been involved.

The next morning, I was sitting at the galley table aboard *Phoenix* with a mug of coffee and a cherry Pop-Tart, working on editing the final chapter of *Stoney's Downfall*. It was clear by then that Jack Stoney had not really fallen down but had only stumbled on his way to solving his case. Bill told me that he only wrote happy endings to his stories because fiction was meant to be an escape from the harsh realities of the real world in which positive outcomes were not guaranteed.

True enough, but I am comfortable with the reality of my life: operating my bar, enjoying Marisa's company, staying in touch with Claire and Jenny, driving around the Sunshine State in my classic Vette with the top down and the music loud, living on my boat with my roomie Joe, staying sober, and enjoying each new day, one at a time. I consider myself to be a rich man. However, I'll admit that it is invigorating to get involved in the occasional murder investigation.

Invigorating.

But only now and then.

33.

A Free Lunch

Seven months had passed since I'd worked The Case of the Dead Philanthropist.

One morning, I was hosing the seagull poop off the deck and roof of *Phoenix* as Joe watched from a safe distance to avoid the spray. Those damn gulls were a constant nuisance whenever they dive-bombed my boat like Japanese Zeros attacking Pearl Harbor on December 7, 1941.

I was just finishing the chore when my cell phone began playing the "Marines' Hymn" in the back pocket of my jeans. I fished it out and saw on the caller ID that it was Cubby Cullen.

"Hey, Cubby," I said when I answered. "What's the latest?"

"Something has come up, Jack," he said. "Let me buy you lunch."

AUTHOR'S NOTE

M y thanks to the folks at The Permanent Press for bringing Detective Jack Starkey to life on the printed page for the third time. Previous books in the series are *Detective Fiction* and *The Dollar-A-Year Detective*. Thanks also to Lon Kirschner for another terrific cover design.

If you are in Boston, the Charlestown Navy Yard is an excellent place to visit. When my wife, Mary, and I lived in Rhode Island, we often went to Boston to shop, eat, and see the sights. A favorite Chinese restaurant of ours was Joyce Chen in Cambridge, now closed. Joyce had a nationally syndicated cooking show on public TV, a series of best-selling cookbooks, and a line of woks. Sometimes we didn't eat there when we'd planned to because we simply could not make our way from downtown Boston to the Harvard Bridge over the Charles River connecting the Back Bay to Cambridge. We joked about hiring a taxi and following it, but never did because there were plenty of good restaurants on the Boston side of the river, including the No Name Restaurant, and Legal Sea Foods, where you can, in fact, get very good scrod.

Anyone familiar with Boston eateries will recognize that Fat Thomas's Tavern is based upon the venerable restaurant Durgin-Park, now, sadly, closed. A story in *USA Today* reported that the restaurant investment group which ended up owning the place decided it was not profitable enough. One of the veteran waitresses was quoted in the story as saying, "This is about greed. It's all about greed . . . the cheap bastards." Surly to the bitter end.

If you are in Chicago, you will not find The Baby Doll Polka Lounge because it does not exist. But there is no shortage of neighborhood bars just like it. And if you do not sample a Chicago-style hot dog at a place like Superdawg Drive-In, a deep-dish pizza at Gino's East, and an Italian beef sandwich at Mr. Beef, and have breakfast at Lou Mitchell's, then you have pretty much wasted your trip.

Although the fictitious Hurricane Irena of this story missed hitting the Southwest Florida Gulf Coast, the real Category 3 Hurricane Irma did make landfall in that location on September 10, 2017. Mary and I and our cat, Oliver, were there, in our house, and took shelter from the storm in a secure location. All of us, and the house, were undamaged, but next time, we'll evacuate. I should have known better. I experienced a hurricane once before. I was aboard the navy destroyer USS *Charles S. Sperry*, DD-697, heading from Newport, Rhode Island, to Guantanamo Bay, Cuba, when we ran into Category 5 Hurricane Camille. If I could have un-joined the navy, I would have, right then. We never made it to Gitmo. We limped back to Newport. The ship was so badly damaged that it was decommissioned and sold to the Chilean Navy. By then, I was safely on shore duty and asked my commanding officer why Chile would want such an unseaworthy ship for its navy. He told me that they couldn't afford much diesel fuel, so they mainly would use it for drills at the pier. I would have preferred that the *Sperry* had remained at the pier while I was aboard.

My cat Lucy, now in cat heaven, and her replacement, Oliver, were the models for Jack Starkey's cat, Joe. They helped me write the three Detective Jack Starkey books—that is, if you can call walking on the keyboard, meowing, and swatting me in the face with their tails, helping.